A Candlelight Ecstasy Romance®

"I THOUGHT YOU WERE MY DATE," DAYRE EXPLAINED.

"But this means . . ." Kenna began to say.

". . . that we've stood up the two people we were supposed to meet," he confirmed. "Do you regret it?"

"I regret not honoring a commitment for dinner," she honestly replied, "but I don't regret meeting you."

"Spoken like a true politician. Let me guess. You're a lady lawyer on her way up in the world, determined to be the first female president."

"Wrong on all counts." She smiled at his stereotyped description. "I'm a high school teacher. How about you?"

"At the moment I'm working as a carpenter."

Kenna's expression was one of surprise. "A carpenter?"

"Something wrong with that?" he challenged.

"No, not at all," she quickly denied, her mind in a whirl. "It must be very rewarding to work with your hands."

He nodded in mocking agreement, letting his gaze wander over her with raw masculine appreciation. "Very rewarding."

CANDLELIGHT ECSTASY ROMANCES®

WINNER
TAKES ALL

Cathie Linz

A CANDLELIGHT ECSTASY ROMANCE®

Published by
Dell Publishing Co., Inc.
1 Dag Hammarskjold Plaza
New York, New York 10017

Dell ® TM 681510, Dell Publishing Co., Inc.

Candlelight Ecstasy Romance®, 1,203,540, is a registered
trademark of Dell Publishing Co., Inc., New York, New
York.

ISBN: 0-440-19529-2

Printed in the United States of America

First printing—September 1984

*To my brother,
the alderman,
who'd better start reading his sister's books!*

*With special thanks
to my state representative
for her invaluable assistance.*

To Our Readers:

We have been delighted with your enthusiastic response to Candlelight Ecstasy Romances®, and we thank you for the interest you have shown in this exciting series.

In the upcoming months we will continue to present the distinctive sensuous love stories you have come to expect only from Ecstasy. We look forward to bringing you many more books from your favorite authors and also the very finest work from new authors of contemporary romantic fiction.

As always, we are striving to present the unique, absorbing love stories that you enjoy most—books that are more than ordinary romance.

Your suggestions and comments are always welcome. Please write to us at the address below.

Sincerely,

The Editors
Candlelight Romances
1 Dag Hammarskjold Plaza
New York, New York 10017

CHAPTER ONE

"Are you still trying to find me the perfect political husband?" Kenna Smith demanded of her campaign manager.

Meg Forrester fixed a reproving look on her chosen candidate while replying with swift affirmation. "Absolutely."

Kenna sighed and slipped off her low-slung pumps. The coolness of the tiled floor provided a welcome relief to her tired, nylon-clad feet. Skipping over the more basic protests, Kenna stated, "I don't have time to get married. Marilyn's got my schedule all booked up for the next umpteen months."

"I think I could squeeze a wedding ceremony in between your luncheon speech to the American Association of University Women and the Meet the Candidate dinner planned by the Chamber of Commerce," Marilyn Preston suggested teasingly.

"You're supposed to be my friend," Kenna grumbled.

Marilyn's grin widened. "I am your friend."

"I know you are," Kenna acknowledged with an answering smile. "You've done wonders arranging my campaign schedule and recruiting volunteers for the primary. I'd be lost without you and Meg."

"Don't mention lost around me," Meg ordered briskly. "We're going to win this primary for the assembly seat, and then we're going to win the election."

"Okay, troops, you've gotten your orders," Marilyn intoned in an imitation of General Patton. "Now, let's go out there and beat the pants off those guys!"

"You've been practicing," Kenna congratulated her. "Do you intend to use that speech at our next staff meeting?"

Kenna's entire campaign staff for a seat in Wisconsin's House of Representatives was composed of friends—politically knowledgeable friends guided by the energetic powerhouse of Meg Forrester.

"May we get back to the matter at hand?" Meg requested.

"I've already told you what I think of this idea," Kenna replied.

"I'll make a deal with you," Meg negotiated. "If this meeting doesn't work out, I'll drop the subject."

"What meeting?"

"The one I've set up for you in"—Meg paused to check her watch—"an hour from now in Madison."

"An hour! That barely gives me time to drive into the city. And it will be rush-hour traffic."

"Most people will be coming out of the city," Meg pointed out, "not driving into it."

Kenna hurriedly slid her shoes back on and then began stuffing papers into her open briefcase. She wanted to study the legislative report on issues pertaining to women tonight, before her speech in front of the Professional Women's Club tomorrow. Consequently her thoughts were on what papers she needed and not entirely on the information Meg was relaying. Certain key words registered.

". . . Arnold's Pub . . . six thirty . . . works for environmental group . . ."

During the hour-long drive south to Madison, Kenna had ample opportunity to reflect on Meg's assertions that being married would help Kenna's chances in the election. It would broaden her level of support and show a sense of stability in her personal life. And so Meg had begun her search for a male marital candidate.

The requirements were precise, right down to age and looks. The prospective candidate had to be older than Kenna's thirty-three years and successful-looking. So far Meg had "fixed her up" with an accountant and a lawyer under the guise of a political meeting. The accountant represented an anti-tax reform lobby and the lawyer a consumer-safety group.

It was six forty by the time Kenna pulled her American-made sedan into the parking lot of Arnold's Pub. She did a rapid check of her appearance in the car's rearview mirror before sliding out of the car and locking it. Her suit had been chosen with durability in mind as well as style, so it showed none of the wrinkles one would have expected to find after a day as hectic as hers had been.

Beyond the sturdy wooden front door the pub's interior was decidedly on the dark side. But even given the poor lighting, Kenna was very much aware of a pair of masculine eyes watching her entrance. Those eyes spoke to her, cutting through the smoke-filled air and honing in on her own searching gaze.

This obviously had to be the man. None of the other men were alone. Walking directly toward him, she held out her hand and said, "Hi, I'm Kenna Smith. Have you been waiting long?"

"No." He took her hand and shook it.

In the course of her campaigning Kenna had shaken countless hands. But none of them had ever produced an electrical aftershock, the likes of which she'd just experienced. Regaining her composure, she smoothly suggested, "Shall we go on in and eat?"

The man hesitated for a moment and then said, "Sure."

Kenna waited until they'd been seated before resuming their conversation. "I'm sorry I'm late," she apologized, rewarding him with a smile.

"No problem." He accepted a menu from the waiter. "I haven't been here that long myself."

"Would you like to order now?" the waiter inquired.

"No. Give us a few minutes to decide."

Pretending to study the menu, Kenna took a moment to size up her dinner companion. The dining area was better lighted than the bar had been and consequently she was able to ascertain that his eyes were a deep, intense blue. Kenna would have killed to own a pair of such thick, dark lashes; her own were pale brown and needed a generous coating of mascara to prevent her from looking like an anemic dishrag.

"Have you decided?" the object of her visual attention looked up to ask.

Yes, I have. This candidate has definite possibilities! Aloud she said, "I'll have the steak."

Once their orders were placed, Kenna invitingly suggested, "Tell me something about yourself, Mr.—"

She paused for a moment, frantically trying to remember the man's name. This kind of lapse, although dreaded, had never struck her before.

"Newport," the man supplied. "D. J. Newport."

"I understand you're interested in environmental matters, Mr. Newport."

"That's right. It appears that you know more about me than I know about you."

Kenna had nothing to hide. "What would you like to know?"

"Let's begin with your name. It's rather unusual."

"My father wanted a son so badly that when he was told he had a daughter, he refused to give up the name he'd chosen—Kenneth. Instead he adapted it to Kenna. What about you? What does D.J. stand for?"

"Dayre Jeremiah." His grimace held a tinge of self-derision. "So you see, I understand all about unusual names."

Kenna laughed, commiserating. "What's the story behind yours?"

"My mother saw the name Dayre on a church notice and liked the look of it. It was only later that she found out the name was supposed to have been Dayrell—the church secretary was a rotten typist!"

While listening to his story, Kenna continued her discreet study of D. J. Newport. She privately thought the name Dayre suited him more than D.J. did. She judged his age to be somewhere between thirty and thirty-five, his height four inches taller than her own five nine. Now that she looked at him closely, she realized that the masculine physique beneath the beige linen jacket was more muscular than either the accountant's or the lawyer's had been.

13

Unlike the other prospective political husbands, Dayre possessed a certain something that intrigued her. Perhaps it was the unusual mixture of humor and pensiveness in his voice. Perhaps it was the so-called Black Irishness of his coloring—dark hair, eyebrows, and lashes, teamed with deep blue eyes. Perhaps it was merely feminine curiosity at the unexpected voltage that had shot up her arm as a result of a simple handshake. Whatever the reason, Kenna found herself contemplating any number of intimate exchanges between herself and one Dayre Jeremiah Newport!

As they passed from course to course, so, too, did their conversation pass from environmental issues to more personal ones. They discovered a mutual aversion to opera and a shared passion for dancing.

Arnold's Pub's fame was not built on the premise of lingering dinners, but rather on high turnover. Consequently the waiter brought their check before they'd even completed their meal. "Is there anything else I can get you?"

"We have everything we need," Dayre replied, keeping his daredevil eyes on Kenna.

He really was a master of speaking looks. The visual means of communication was somehow more intimately expressive than the spoken word. Kenna, accustomed to the conversational technique of establishing eye contact during a discussion, was unaccustomed to the resultant wake of warmth produced by even a brushing glance of his blue eyes. But then the chemistry had clicked between them from the very beginning, when she'd first seen him, his gaze catching hers across the crowded bar.

"If you're ready, I'll take that for you," the waiter said, interrupting the couple's visual immersion.

"I get the impression we're holding things up," Kenna noted as their hovering waiter gathered up the check and the credit card Dayre had tossed on top of it.

When Dayre held out his hand to Kenna as she stood up, she put her own into it without a moment's hesitation. The physical link, small though it was, established a new line of communication. A pleasurable thrill radiated from their linked fingers, up her arm, to her heart, where it kicked her pulse rate into overdrive.

The daredevil flare in his eyes told her that he, too, felt the magic brewing between them. "Let's dance."

"There's no music," she was sorry to have to say.

"Then we'll go across the street. Madigan's has dancing every night."

"Sir . . ." their waiter reminded Dayre, "you have to sign here."

Dayre signed the receipt and grabbed his credit card from the plastic clipboard. "Let's go." He placed a guiding hand at Kenna's back as they wove their way out of the popular eatery.

Across the street Madigan's was just as crowded. The band was playing surprisingly slow music. Catching sight of Kenna's expression, Dayre teased, "What did you expect? Slam dancing?"

"I didn't realize people still danced this way."

"It's the only way," he murmured. "Shall we?"

"I'd love to."

Going into his arms gave her a peculiar sense of

15

homecoming. His broad shoulders offered her chin a tempting resting place. Her eyes closed in an attempt to overcome temptation. It didn't work.

There was no getting away from the fact that her senses were finely tuned to the slightest movement of her partner. She could feel him breathing, feel the steady pumping of his heart beneath her hand. Heat radiated from his arm, which encircled her lower back.

Her fingers slid over his linen jacket, appreciating the shifting flow of muscles beneath its nubby texture. Unable to resist temptation any longer, Kenna allowed her chin to brush against his shoulder before settling there. She'd given in to one temptation only to be faced with another. Now her fingers were a mere inch from the nape of his neck and the dark thickness of his hair.

Dayre reacted to the new closeness of their embrace by resting his chin against her temple, so that they were dancing cheek-to-cheek. Both of his arms now circled her waist, communicating his desire. They remained on the dance floor, using the music as an excuse to stay in each other's arms, until the band switched to a new wave beat.

When they returned to their table they lingered over their after-dinner drinks.

"I'd like to propose a toast," Dayre declared. The slow sweep of his eyes down her face and body was more potent than the alcohol in their glasses. "Let's drink to the person who brought us together tonight."

"Good idea," she murmured.

Lifting their glasses they simultaneously toasted "To . . ."

". . . Meg!" said Kenna.

". . . Cindy!" said Dayre.

CHAPTER TWO

"Who's Cindy?" Kenna was asking while Dayre demanded, "Who's Meg?"

Kenna's forehead wrinkled into a frown and she cautiously lowered her drink, as if fearing that it might be responsible for the confusion between them. "Meg is my campaign manager."

"Campaign?" Dayre immediately honed in on the key word. "As in political campaign?"

"That's right. I'm running to fill a vacancy in the state assembly. Meg arranged this meeting tonight so that we could discuss some of the state's environmental issues. . . ." Kenna trailed off as Dayre shook his head.

"Meg didn't arrange this meeting," he said. "Not between you and me."

"I'm afraid I don't understand," she answered. Actually she was afraid she *did* understand and didn't want to have to face reality quite yet.

"I wasn't at Arnold's to meet Kenna Smith, political candidate. I was there to meet a blind date set up for me by my matchmaking sister, Cindy," he stated bluntly.

Feeling like an idiot, she demanded, "Then why did you look at me as if you were expecting me?"

Dayre muttered something that sounded like "I've been expecting you for years," before saying, "I thought you were my date."

"But this means . . ."

". . . that we've stood up the two people we were supposed to meet," he confirmed. "Do you regret it?"

"I regret not honoring a commitment for dinner," she honestly replied, "but I don't regret meeting you."

"Spoken like a true politician." His brow rose mockingly. "Let me guess. You're a lady lawyer on her way up in the world, determined to be the first female president."

"Wrong on all counts." She smiled at his stereotyped description. "I'm a high school teacher. How about you?"

Dayre took a healthy swig of his drink before answering, "At the moment I'm working as a carpenter."

Kenna's expression was one of surprise. "A carpenter?"

"Something wrong with that?" he challenged.

"No, not at all," she quickly replied, her mind in a whirl. This explained the calluses she'd felt on his hands, the calluses she'd attributed to racquetball or tennis, not manual labor! At a loss for words, she lamely said, "It must be very rewarding to work with your hands."

He nodded in mocking agreement, letting his gaze wander over her with raw masculine appreciation. "Very rewarding."

Kenna eyed him warily, feeling as if the wolf had

suddenly stepped out of its sheep's clothing. "I want you to know that I don't make a habit out of picking up strange men in bars," she heard herself say with uncharacteristic awkwardness.

Dayre hitched his chair closer and asked with enthusiastic interest, "Where do you pick up strange men?"

"I don't pick them at all," Kenna returned with her more customary élan. "I leave them on the tree."

A grin slashed its way across his face, warming his blue eyes with specks of light. "Nicely said, Kenna Smith."

She smiled in return and said, "Thank you."

"Shall we resume our toast?"

"Certainly." She reached for her drink.

"To serendipity," he murmured, touching her glass with his.

The intensity of his gaze was so strong that Kenna couldn't pull her eyes away from it. No one else had ever looked at her in quite that way, communicating a wealth of hidden messages too intense to be deciphered. Kenna had never considered herself to be the susceptible kind, but those eyes of his did sinful things to her!

Her tongue flicked out to dampen her bone-dry lips. Her eyes were freed from their captivity as his gaze lowered to her mouth, focusing on her lips with a determined absorption as forceful as a kiss. His thoughts might as well have been printed on his brow, so clearly did she see them. Dayre was imagining kissing her. Her breathing became shallow and light as she, too, joined in the mind game, allowing her fantasies to develop.

Would his lips be cool or warm, smooth or rough? Would he taste her in bites or devour her all at once? Would he be a passionate lover? Would his lovemaking be slow and tender? Evocative and sexy? Wild and primitive? Tumultuous and exhilarating?

Her trembling fingers sent the forgotten drink in her raised hand sloshing over the edge of the glass, soaking her hand. The incident belatedly recalled Kenna to reality, breaking her trancelike state.

As soon as she lowered her glass to the table, Dayre took possession of her hand and daringly lifted it to his lips. His tongue darted out to lick the alcohol from her fingers. His cleansing ministrations went from fingertip to knuckle with sweeping strokes. When the tip of his tongue insinuated itself between her fingers, probing the ultrasensitive skin, Kenna could only gasp with pleasure.

"Intoxicating," Dayre murmured, whether in reference to her taste or her response, she couldn't be sure.

"It's getting late," she said in a half-strangled voice.

He released her hand with a regretful sigh. "All right, we'll leave. But I have no intention of letting you get away from me." His low voice proclaimed his determination. "I want to see you again."

Kenna would have been less than honest had she not admitted that she wanted to see him again also. Since, as those who knew her well would testify, Kenna was *exceedingly* honest, she readily agreed. "Okay."

"Okay?" Dayre repeated. He had expected her to put up at least a token sign of resistance and her ready agreement momentarily surprised him.

"Sure." When Kenna smiled her entire face lit up.

21

"I feel it's my civic duty to prove to you that politicians can be trustworthy!"

"Civic duty, huh?" He traced the curve of her jaw with a surprisingly gentle hand.

"Among other things," she murmured, turning her face up to his.

"It's the other things that interest me," he stated huskily. "Come on, I'll walk you to your car."

The parking lot at Arnold's Pub was well lit, but Kenna made no protest as Dayre insisted on escorting her right to her car. "Thank you for a lovely evening," she said, her sincerity transforming the polite cliché into something personal.

"It's only the first of many," he replied, taking the keys from her hand and unlocking the car door for her. "Tell me where your campaign office is, and I'll pick you up there tomorrow night."

She gave him the instructions, adding, "I've got meetings and personal appearances set up all day. I won't be free until six thirty or seven."

"I'll be there at seven." Dayre paused as she shivered slightly from the cool night breeze. "It's chilly out here." He gently grasped the lapels of her suit jacket, joining them together in the front. "I wouldn't want you to catch cold." He slid his fingers beneath the jacket's collar and turned it up against the nape of her neck. "Better?" he asked softly, his hand still holding on to her collar.

"Much," she replied huskily, moved by the gentleness of his powerful hands.

"Maybe I should share a little of my body heat. . . ." With each word he said he drew her an inch closer, gazing into her eyes all the while. The fiery

22

hunger in his eyes held enough thermal energy to warm all of Madison, so it was no surprise to Kenna that it melted her.

His mouth lowered to hers with smooth deliberation, hovering over her parted lips like a bee courting a flower. His hands pulled her closer to him, erasing the provocative space between them. His kiss, when it came, was an evocative sampling of light grazes and tempting brushes that left room for discovery. Compared to the often smothering first kisses Kenna had received in the past, this mutual exploration was incredibly tantalizing.

Wanting to taste more, Kenna moved closer, resting her hands on his waist. Her responsiveness was rewarded by a deepening of the kiss. His tongue took the promise she offered, slipping past her parted lips, leaving no portion of her mouth unexplored.

Powerful crosscurrents of emotion coursed through her, blocking out everything but this expansive pleasure. It took the arrival of a rowdy bunch of teenagers to tear them apart. Even after he released her, she was still left with a lingering warmth that stayed with her during the drive home.

The phone was ringing as Kenna let herself into her town house. Her thoughts were on Dayre as she answered.

"Kenna, do you have any idea what time it is?" Meg demanded.

Kenna checked her watch before saying, "You called me at one forty-three to ask what time it is?"

Meg didn't bother answering Kenna's teasing question. Instead, she got right to the point. "Where have you been?"

"Out to dinner."

"All this time?"

Kenna smiled and kicked off her shoes. "Meg, I'm a little old to have a curfew."

"How did it go?"

"I think I've found Mr. Right," Kenna replied dreamily.

"Larry Laruda?"

"No." Kenna tangled her finger in the coiled phone wire, a reminiscing smile curving her lips. "Dayre Newport."

"Who's Dayre Newport?" Meg demanded in confusion.

"A man I met at Arnold's Pub."

"I sent you there to meet Larry Laruda."

"I know," Kenna acknowledged, stifling a yawn. "It's a long story. I'll tell you all about it in the morning."

Meg made sure that she did, confronting Kenna the moment she came into the office. "Start at the beginning and tell me everything that happened."

"Everything?" Kenna mocked with a raised brow.

"Everything," Meg repeated.

"There was a mix-up when I arrived at the restaurant. The man I met turned out to be the wrong one."

"Last night you claimed he was Mr. Right."

"He is. I meant wrong only as far as *you* were concerned."

"I think she's warning you off him," Marilyn said as she joined them.

"Come on, Kenna," Meg sighed. "You're not usually this inarticulate."

"Must have been her late night out," Marilyn suggested.

"It boils down to a simple case of mistaken identity. I thought Dayre was the man you intended me to meet."

"But *Dayre Newport* doesn't sound anything like *Larry Laruda*," Meg retorted. "How could you get them mixed up?"

"I didn't remember Larry Laruda's name. All I remembered you saying was the time and place of the meeting, and the fact that we would be discussing environmental issues. Dayre and I did discuss environmental issues." *Among other things,* she silently added, to which she could almost hear his reply. *It's the other things that interest me.*

Marilyn interrupted Kenna's daydreaming to ask, "What does this Dayre Newport do for a living?"

"He's a carpenter."

Meg paused a moment, her eyes narrowed in thought. "Can he bring out the labor vote?"

"Can he fix my roof?" Marilyn inserted.

"In reply to the first question, Dayre doesn't live in my district, so I don't think there's much chance of him bringing in the labor vote. As to the second, I don't know if he can fix your roof, Marilyn. You'll have to ask him yourself. He'll be stopping by here tonight."

"Tonight? But you've got a five thirty meeting with the representatives from Citizens for Churches."

"Dayre's stopping by after that. He said around seven."

"Enough of this small talk," Meg decided. "Did you

finish your outline for your luncheon speech for the American Association of University Women?"

After confirming that she had, Kenna launched into a practice run, competently and concisely answering the questions Meg posed to her. The rehearsal stood Kenna in good stead and her speech was enthusiastically welcomed.

Her schedule left no time for thoughts of Dayre and their upcoming evening together. After her luncheon speech she made four personal appearances at local shopping centers, meeting constituents and shaking hands before returning to the office for the meeting with the ecclesiastical representatives.

At seven o'clock Kenna, Meg, and Marilyn were all standing before a detailed map of the district. They were plotting out those areas where door-to-door campaigning would have the most impact, when the door to their small storefront office opened.

"Am I interrupting something?" Dayre asked.

Kenna immediately turned to face him, eager to see him after her long day. Her eyes widened as she took in his appearance. Work boots covered his feet and the lower edges of his well-washed jeans. His light blue denim workshirt was clean but equally faded, while a Levi jacket was casually slung over one shoulder. Topping it all off was a New York Mets baseball cap on his head!

"Dayre Newport, I presume?" Meg questioned on the edge of a laugh.

"Call me D.J.," Dayre instructed her, moving toward Meg to accept her offer of a handshake.

Meg wasn't put off by Dayre's casual appearance or introduction. Here was a man who knew his goals in life and was meeting them. It showed in the way he carried himself, in the self-assurance of his handclasp. "D.J. it is," she agreed, her doubts having been cleared by her rapid character assessment. "You can call me Meg."

"You don't look anything like a campaign manager," he reflected, scrutinizing the dynamic Meg from her wiry gray hair to her well-shod feet.

"Dayre has this problem with stereotyping," Kenna explained.

"She's trying to cure me," he tacked on. "So if you'll excuse us, we'll go begin lesson one." With ingenious expediency he took Kenna's arm and led her out of the office.

"What do you think?" Meg asked Marilyn.

"He's a smooth mover. One look at him and I forgot all about leaky roofs!"

"I just hope Kenna doesn't forget about the demands of this campaign." Meg sounded worried.

Marilyn's expression turned serious. "You know you can count on Kenna no matter what extenuating circumstances may come her way. Even one as good-looking as D.J. Besides, you're the one who's been pushing her to get married."

"To someone who would help her political aspirations," Meg qualified.

"You don't think D.J. is the right man for her?" Marilyn questioned.

"I'm afraid he may well be the right man for her. I'd just like to know a little more about him."

Down the street Kenna and Dayre were standing on the street corner beside her parked car.

"Your car or mine?" he asked, pointing to a red Bronco parked across the street.

"I guess that depends on where we're going."

"If I get to pick the place, then I choose your place."

Kenna stared at him with blank surprise. "My place?"

"You do have one, don't you?"

"Well, yes, but . . ."

"Then lead on. I'll follow you in the Bronco."

"What about eating? I'm starving."

His gaze focused on her mouth as he concurred, "So am I."

"I was talking about food."

"So was I," he insisted innocently.

"I don't have anything to eat at home."

"Then we'll just stop somewhere along the way and pick up something to eat."

Half an hour later, with a bucket of barbecued ribs in hand, Dayre stood in her living room looking around with interest. "It looks like you," he decided.

"I look like a piece of furniture?" she mocked, taking the bucket of food from him and setting it on a round butcher-block table.

"The Scandinavian style looks like you. Must be your blond hair and blue eyes."

"My mother was Swedish," Kenna related.

"Your mother?"

"She died when I was seven. What about your parents?" she went on to ask before he could offer his sympathies.

"Mom and Pop are up in Alaska."

"Are they there on vacation or do they live there?"

"Neither. They're working."

"Working?"

"With the Eskimos."

"I see," she said, even though she didn't. Strolling over to her refrigerator, she asked, "Umm, what would you like to drink with our meal?"

"What've you got?"

"Not much." She studied the uninspiring contents before closing the door. "There's a bottle of wine here somewhere, but it's not chilled."

"Ever heard of ice cubes?"

"Ah-hah! Here's the wine." She triumphantly held the bottle aloft. "Now for the ice cubes." Turning to open the freezer door, she became aware of Dayre's steady gaze on her. His warm intensity threw her. "I'm sorry it's so hot in here, I forgot to turn on the air conditioner this morning. It's awful warm for June, isn't it?" The realization that she was babbling brought a tint of color to her face.

"You do look warm," Dayre commented. He snitched one of the ice cubes from her tray and held it up to her face. Gently gliding it across her flushed face, he asked, "Better?"

"Much," she replied. Closing her eyes further excited her senses. The heady combination of his warm fingers and the cold ice cube provoked feverish chills running up and down her spine. Her eyes popped open as something else slid down her spine, the ice cube! Her shriek of shock superseded Dayre's apology.

"I'm sorry, it slipped. Here, let me help." He reached behind her to tug the blouse from her skirt.

"What are you doing?" she cried.

"Capturing your runaway ice cube." He slid his

29

hand beneath the blouse, his fingers burning on her bare skin before sliding away, ice cube in hand. "I got the devil."

"I think the devil is standing right in front of me," Kenna retorted tartly, briskly tucking her blouse back in.

"You think I did that on purpose?" he marveled with exaggerated pain, dropping the melting ice cube into the sink.

"I *think* we'd better eat," she answered.

"How's the campaigning going?" Dayre asked a few minutes later as he bit into a tangy rib.

"Today things went fairly well," Kenna answered, sucking barbecue sauce from her thumb. "The speech I gave this afternoon received an enthusiastic response."

"What did you talk about?"

"Women's issues."

"And did the rally end with a flurry of bra burnings?"

"Shame, shame." She shook her head at him. Had Dayre been serious in his scorn of women's rights, he would now be standing on the other side of her front door! But Kenna knew the male psyche well enough to recognize baiting when she heard it. Dayre obviously enjoyed playing the devil's advocate.

"You're falling behind the times," she chastised him gently. "Bra burning dates back to the seventies. We're now in the eighties, in case someone failed to notify you of that fact."

His face fell with disappointment. "Does that mean there was no bra burning?"

"You catch on fast."

He returned the compliment. "So do you."

She knew he was referring to her recognition of his baiting techniques. "Does that bother you?"

"No. Should it?"

"No. Not since you really aren't what you're pretending to be."

A strange look of discomfiture momentarily flashed in his eyes. "What do you mean by that?"

"Simply that I don't believe you're really a male chauvinist. If I did, you wouldn't be eating here tonight."

He grinned, almost as if in relief before casually asking, "What gave me away?"

"I think I'd have to say it was your eyes."

"My eyes?"

"They had a gleam of humor instead of fanaticism."

"I can see I'll have to watch myself around you. The problem is—when I am around you, I'd rather watch you."

The feeling, Kenna silently mused, *could well be mutual.* When near Dayre, she found it hard to keep her eyes off him.

"So tell me, how does a schoolteacher get to be a politician?" Dayre asked.

"I'm not a politician yet," she corrected him. "I'm a candidate."

"You wouldn't happen to teach English, by any chance, would you?" he teased.

"I'm the head of the English Department, actually. How did you know?"

"Just a wild guess." He shrugged with a knowing grin.

"Come on, tell me," she coaxed. "What gave me away?"

He repeated her answer by saying, "Your eyes."

"I suppose next you're going to tell me they have commas and semicolons written on them."

"Now, don't go all grammatical on me," he laughed, his voice flowing over her.

Kenna felt the force of his magnetism, and tried to shake off the powerful tug of attraction by prosaically reaching for the last barbecued rib. Dayre had the same idea in mind, and their fingers met in the tangy sauce. Kenna jerked her hand away nervously, and ended up knocking her knife to the floor.

"I'll get it," she quickly stated before Dayre could offer to do so. The stainless steel piece of cutlery had fallen out of her reach. She leaned over just a little bit farther and the award-winning Breuer chair she was sitting on rocked forward, tipping her onto the carpet.

She didn't have time to recover before Dayre was on his knees beside her. "Are you all right?" he asked in concern.

"Aside from being acutely embarrassed, you mean?" she muttered, attempting to scramble to her feet. But a pair of masculine hands restrained her.

"I suppose if you're not the kind of woman who picks up strange men in bars, it would be too much to hope that you make a practice of finagling your male guests to the floor for a bit of romantic wrestling, huh?" His expression was wistful and it made Kenna laugh. "Hey, you're not supposed to laugh at me when I'm flirting with you," he chastised her with a reprimanding tap on her nose.

"I'm too old and too tall to flirt," she scoffed dryly.

"How old are you?" he questioned, showing no sign of letting her up from the carpet.

"Thirty-three," she answered.

"There you go. I'm several inches taller, and a year older than you are. If I can flirt, so can you," he stated, sealing his logical proclamation with a kiss. "You taste better than the ribs," he leaned back to murmur.

Seeing the warm response in her eyes, he rubbed the ball of his thumb over her damp lips, parting them ever so slightly. His eyes never left her as his head lowered to taste the response he'd viewed.

Adjusting to the now familiar shape of his body, her mouth curved into a smile of pleasure, a pleasure that intensified as his tongue engaged hers in an erotic skirmish. Her head bent back beneath the hungry pressure of their kiss as hot sparks jumped along her spine and curled her toes. When his thumb angled the curve of her jaw to change the slant of her mouth, Kenna eagerly complied.

With his body covering hers, Kenna marveled at the perfect fit of her femininity to his masculinity. His questing fingers marveled at the same thing, surveying the rounded softness of her hip, the inverted curve of her waist, the tender thrust of her breasts, with skillful expertise. A wave of primitive emotion rocked her body and sent her own fingers in search of new masculine territory to conquer.

Kenna's hands rode up his back and ran down his spine. Beneath the warm denim shirt was even warmer skin. His shoulders were broad, his waist trim, his hips narrow. She knew the feel of each as she explored the wonders of his body. Only when desire throbbed in

33

time to their pounding hearts did she realize the danger of such intimate liberties.

Dayre became equally aware of his own imminent loss of control and reluctantly set her loose. Rolling to his feet with the ease of a man in perfect shape, he ran distracted fingers through his already tousled hair. His Mets baseball cap had long since been discarded.

Kenna scrambled to her feet. "I'm sorry about that."

"Don't be."

"I never meant . . ."

He stilled her words with a silencing finger. "Lady, you may not flirt," he growled with shaky humor, "but as far as I'm concerned, when it comes to romantic wrestling—you're an expert!"

CHAPTER THREE

"How did it go last night?" Marilyn questioned Kenna the next morning.

"Great," Kenna replied with a somewhat dreamy version of her usual smile.

"Great? That's all you're going to tell me?"

"That's all," Kenna confirmed. On the verge of turning away, she added, "Oh, and Marilyn . . ."

"Yes?"

"Dayre doesn't do roofs!"

The storefront campaign office was busy all morning. Only the size of Kenna's living room, this space had been donated to them by Marilyn's husband, Ron, who owned the hardware store next door. Kenna's so-called private office was actually a corner of the otherwise open area, isolated from the noise and organized chaos by a pair of wicker screens and consisting of an old oak desk and two straight-back chairs.

Kenna spent an hour each morning studying the latest legislative reports published by the state. Meg normally made it a point not to interrupt during these study sessions, but today she had a visitor she wasn't sure what to do with.

"Kenna, there's someone here to see you," Meg announced before coming around the screen.

Kenna looked up in surprise. She wasn't expecting anyone. Unless Dayre . . . But it wasn't Dayre who stood beside Meg. This man was equally tall but had light hair instead of dark. He was also exceptionally good-looking.

"Kenna, I'd like you to meet Larry Laruda."

So this was the man she was supposed to have met! Marital candidate number three! Kenna stood up and offered him her hand. "I'm sorry about the mix-up in our appointment the other evening, Mr. Laruda."

His grip was firm, but it did nothing for her as he shook her hand. Why was it that this hunk of masculinity left her cold while Dayre melted her to the core?

"Actually I'm the one who should apologize, Ms. Smith," Larry countered smoothly. "My car broke down on the way to the pub. By the time I got there, you must have already left. I waited around the bar for a while, but there was no sign of you."

That's because I was probably eating in the restaurant with Dayre, Kenna supplied silently.

"Perhaps we can discuss your views on the state's environment now?" Larry suggested.

Kenna checked the open appointment book lying on her desk before nodding affirmatively. "I've got some time."

Larry presented his environmental position with clear and concise terminology. He knew his field and made it a point not to cloud the issues with an overuse of statistics. Listening to him, Kenna couldn't help but wonder at the night-and-day difference between her reaction to Dayre and her reaction to Larry. Of the two, she'd have to say that Larry was the more traditionally good-looking. His credentials were superb, his manner charming. But nothing clicked between them.

"I'm glad to see we agree on so many points," Larry smiled. "Would you care to continue this discussion over lunch?"

"Lunch is already booked, I'm afraid. A speech at the Rotary."

"Mind if I tag along?" Larry asked.

"Not at all. I should warn you though that I'm not going to be discussing the environment," she teased with a smile.

"Kenna, there's a call for you on line one," Marilyn called out.

"Thanks," she called back, adding in a quieter tone, "Excuse me a moment, Larry." Punching the appropriate button, she said, "Kenna Smith here."

"I know, and I wish she were here with me instead," Dayre's dark voice murmured.

"What can I do for you?" Kenna knew the automatic question was a mistake the moment she said it.

Dayre made the most of it, his low-pitched laughter disturbingly seductive as he murmured, "I can think of any number of things."

"I'm sure you can," she acknowledged wryly. Seeing Larry's miming motion to his watch, she answered, "I'll be right there, Larry."

"Larry?" Dayre repeated suspiciously.

"Larry Laruda. He works for the Environmental . . ."

"I know who he works for," Dayre interrupted, his tone holding a new sense of purpose. "Kenna, there's something I have to tell you."

37

"I'm afraid it will have to wait," Kenna had to say. "I'm late already."

"When will you be back?" he demanded, not at all pleased.

"About two thirty," she calculated.

"I'll call you then." He made it sound like a royal proclamation.

The Rotary lunch didn't last as long as she'd expected and Kenna was back in her campaign office by just after two. "I'm looking for Kenna Smith," a man in coveralls stated hesitatingly.

"You've found her," Kenna replied. "What can I do for you?"

"My name is Harry Conley. I'm D.J.'s brother-in-law. I was doing some work in the area—thought I'd stop by and meet you."

"I'm glad to meet you, Mr. Conley."

"Call me Harry," he instructed her.

"Harry it is," she obliged. "Come on into my office, Harry. Would you like some coffee?"

"No, thanks," he refused her, taking a seat on one of the straight-back chairs. "D.J.'s told us a lot about you."

Kenna took her place behind the desk. "He has?"

"Sure thing. Cindy, that's my wife, couldn't believe the mix-up at the pub. She's the one who set up the blind date, you know."

Kenna nodded. "I know."

"Of course when D.J. told us you were a lady politician we thought he was pulling our leg. Not that D.J. isn't respectable enough for a politician," Harry assured her hastily. "Cindy's the black sheep in the family, but D.J.'s a real chip off the old block. Just like his father."

"His father is a carpenter too?"

"A carpenter?" Harry repeated in astonishment. "No, D.J.'s father is a professor of anthropology. Dr. Newport and his wife are up in Alaska now, working with the Eskimos. Mind you, D.J.'s only an associate professor at U of W, but their engineering school is one of the best in the country. Did you know that?"

Kenna shook her head. Apparently there was a lot about Dayre that she didn't know!

"We knew when he graduated at the top of his class that D.J. would go far. Cindy was so pleased to have him close to home again, what with their parents traveling so much. For a while there she was afraid D.J. was going to really follow in his father's footsteps and wander around the world. But now he's showing real signs of settling down right here in Madison. But he's probably told you all this himself."

"No, actually he hasn't," Kenna replied in a slow drawl.

"Isn't that just like D.J.? He's awful modest about his accomplishments. In fact, none of my construction crew even know that D.J. is really a professor. They think he's just a carpenter, if you can believe that!"

"Oh, I can believe it," Kenna murmured. *At the moment, I'm a carpenter,* he replied when she'd asked about his livelihood at their first meeting. Knowing Dayre's wide streak of perversity, Kenna didn't get angry at his deception. But she certainly had no intention of allowing him to get away with it either!

"Harry, I wonder if I could ask a favor of you?"

"Sure. Shoot."

39

"I'm afraid your brother-in-law has been having a little fun at my expense."

Harry looked uncomfortable. "Come again?"

"Dayre told me he was a carpenter," she stated bluntly.

"You mean D.J. used his carpenter routine on you too?"

Kenna nodded. "And I'd like your help in paying him back."

"I don't know about that," Harry protested.

"It's all right," she assured him with dry humor. "I'm not suggesting anything violent. You said that no one on the construction crew knows Dayre's a professor?"

"That's right. D.J. thought it might make the men uncomfortable. This way he can just be one of the guys. And no one calls him Dayre," Harry felt obliged to tack on.

"Why not?" Kenna asked, even though she imagined she already knew the answer.

"Because he's not very fond of his full name. You can imagine what the other guys' reaction would be to a hardhat named Dayre."

"Yes, I can," she agreed with a satisfied smile. "And that reaction is precisely what I'm aiming to use as punishment."

"You mean you want to blow D.J.'s cover?"

"Absolutely." Kenna rose from her chair to come around the desk and perch on its corner. "Will you help me?" she asked with appealing directness.

"D.J. will be madder than hell if I do," Harry murmured his thoughts aloud. "But, then, he'll already be mad that I ruined his carpenter routine with you.

Okay," he decided with firm resolution. "I'll help. What do you want me to do?"

"You said something about being in the area to do some work," she prompted.

"That's right," Harry confirmed. "We're starting work on a building a block east of here."

"Perfect! When are you beginning the project?"

"Tomorrow."

"Will Dayre be working there?"

"If he has anything to say about it, he will. He already put in a bid to work here, said something about this area fascinating him." Harry's mocking inflection told her that he clearly thought she was the object of Dayre's fascination.

"I think he will find this area worthy of fascination!" Her smile turned into an anticipatory grin. "I'll swing by the work site tomorrow and pay one Dayre Jeremiah Newport a visit."

"I'll supply the hard hat," Harry chuckled.

Kenna frowned. "Is it a heavy construction area?"

"Not really, but the . . . ah . . . manure," he delicately ventured, "will really hit the fan when D.J. finds out about this!"

"I'll pass," Kenna returned with a grin. "If the . . . ah . . . manure does hit the fan, I don't think a hard hat will provide much protection!"

Marilyn interrupted them to say, "Kenna, there's a call for you. It's Dayre."

"I've gotta get going anyway," Harry decided. "I'll see you tomorrow, Kenna. And watch your step."

"I will. Thanks, Harry."

She left her perch on the desk to answer the phone. "Hi, Dayre. You caught me on my way out again."

"You just got there," he accused her.

"I told you my schedule is hectic. It's all in a day in the life of a politician."

"You're a candidate," he corrected her as she had corrected him earlier.

"Candidates' schedules are even worse."

"You've got an answer for everything, don't you?"

"Not quite." For example, she didn't know what she was going to say to him tomorrow, but it would be something guaranteed to put a dent in that hard-hat image of his! Anticipation of the event made her say, "But I'm working on it."

"I'm going to be up in your neighborhood tomorrow. How about lunch? Unless you're speaking to the 4-H Club or some other worthy organization?" he added with deliberate mockery.

"The 4-H Club is Thursday," she had a hard time saying with a straight face. "So lunch tomorrow will be fine."

Detecting something suspicious in her tone, Dayre demanded, "Are you going to be seeing Larry Laruda again before tomorrow?"

"I have no plans to," she honestly replied. "Why?"

"No reason," he dismissed. "I'll see you tomorrow."

Kenna hung up the phone with a jaunty smile and when it was safe added a soft, "Yes, you will, Professor Newport!"

"You look like the cat that ate the canary," Marilyn observed as Kenna came out of her private office. "What gives?"

"Where's Meg?" Kenna countered in a tantalizing way. "I don't want to go over this twice."

"Go over what twice?" Marilyn complained, following Kenna across the office as she spotted Meg.

"I'd like to call a mini-powwow in my cubicle," Kenna announced.

In reply to Meg's questioning glance, Marilyn could only shrug.

"Is there some problem?" Meg inquired once they were all seated.

"Only if your name is Dayre Newport," Kenna replied.

"That lets me out." Marilyn grinned.

"Me too," Meg concurred. "Care to tell us what this is all about?"

Kenna made the announcement. "It seems our favorite carpenter is actually an associate professor of engineering at the University of Wisconsin."

Meg leaned back with a satisfied smile while Marilyn leaned forward with an impressed whistle. "A professor! Why's he disguising himself as a carpenter?"

"Masculine perversity," Kenna diagnosed dryly. "He's going to be out here working in this area tomorrow and I thought I'd pay him a little visit. It seems our carpenter likes to hide his light under a bushel, and consequently no one on the construction crew knows about his academic background."

"The College of Engineering is one of the best in the country," Meg noted.

"So I've been told. Do you think you could do me a favor, Meg, and check out Professor Dayre Newport? I'd like to know more about him and thereby prevent any further surprises."

"Actually, I already started nosing around," Meg had to admit.

"And?" Kenna demanded.

Meg checked her clipboard. "No criminal record."

"That's reassuring."

"Single."

"Also reassuring!"

"That's about all I've got so far. I'll check with the university and see what I can find from there."

Kenna didn't have to warn Meg to be discreet; anyone who could arrange three meetings for prospective political husbands without a hint of scandal had to be discreet!

"What excuse are you going to use for dropping by the construction site?" Marilyn questioned.

"Dayre's invited me to lunch."

"He's obviously going to get more than he bargained for!" Marilyn forecast accurately.

Kenna found the building site the next day without any difficulty. Harry was stationed near the building's entrance, as he'd promised to be. "D.J.'s upstairs," he informed her in a conspiratorial whisper.

"Thanks, Harry." She rewarded him with several pieces of the homemade fried chicken Marilyn had donated to the cause.

With basket in hand, she headed for the flight of stairs. Halfway up she cried out, "Yoo-hoo! Is Professor Dayre Jeremiah Newport up there?"

The sound of a hammer crashing to the floor was immediately followed by the muffled sound of swearing. By the time she reached the top of the steps, she saw Dayre standing near the windows. The sunlight gleamed on the sweat-slicked skin of his bare chest, highlighting the ripple of his muscles. He looked like a

Greek sculpture, except for the fact that he had the thumb of his left hand stuck in his mouth!

"You really shouldn't bite your nails, Professor," she chastised him.

"Professor?" a man working on the plumbing repeated.

"That's right," Kenna confirmed. "Professor Dayre Jeremiah Newport, University of Wisconsin."

"Dare?" said one worker.

"Jeremiah?" choked another.

Dayre's brows lowered threateningly as he immediately removed his injured thumb from his mouth. "What are you doing here?" he growled at Kenna.

"I've brought a little something for you to eat. Lunch. There's enough for everyone," she declared as she invited the construction crew to join them.

The tempting aroma beckoned the other men close.

"Smells like chicken," one man claimed.

"Fried chicken," another clarified.

"Hey, Newport, aren't you going to introduce us?" a third demanded.

"Jimmy, Sam, Danny, Merv, Tony—this is Kenna Smith."

Kenna nodded to each of the men. "Here, let me take that heavy basket," Jimmy offered. Or was it Tony? Dayre had made the introductions so rapidly that Kenna couldn't be sure.

The man, whatever his name, relieved her of the basket and put it on what looked like a door placed horizontally between two sawhorses. Daintily stepping over sawdust-coated two-by-fours, Kenna followed him. The rest of the men clamored around her as she proceeded to pass out paper plates full of delicious chicken, talking nonstop all the while.

"You guys must be starving after working so hard. Here, have another piece of chicken, there's plenty left. It's a shame Dayre isn't joining us."

"Hey, Newport, you didn't tell us she could cook," Danny kidded.

When a couple of the men popped up with variations of "This is great, Kenna," Dayre growled, "It's Ms. Smith to you gorillas."

"Touchy, touchy, Dayre," the guys laughed.

"I'm afraid these academic types are like that," Kenna sighed.

That did it! Dayre strode across the room and grabbed her elbow. "We have to talk." He sounded furious. "Somewhere more private." He attempted to hustle her toward the stairs.

But at five nine Kenna was hard to hustle, unless she chose to be hustled. She stood her ground. "How sweet, Dayre." She patted his hand, the one that had a stranglehold on her arm. "But that's not necessary. I only stopped by for a minute. I have to be on my way." Turning to her eager audience of construction workers, she added, "I hope I can count on you boys to make sure Dayre here eats his share."

A moment later she was free and Dayre was surrounded by burly bodies. "I'm allergic to crow!" Dayre valiantly maintained as, with a cheery wave of her hand, Kenna made her escape, leaving him in the capable clutches of his coworkers.

CHAPTER FOUR

"Who told you?" Dayre demanded when he caught up with her on the corner of the block. "Larry?"

"Larry?" she repeated in confusion. Had that been the electrician or the plumber on Dayre's work crew?

"Laruda," Dayre impatiently jogged her memory.

"What does Larry Laruda have to do with this?" Kenna asked in confusion.

"You tell me."

"As far as I know, he has nothing to do with this."

"If Larry didn't tell you then who? Harry!" Dayre breathed with dawning comprehension.

"Let's get back to Larry here for a minute. Are you telling me you two know each other?"

"We roomed together in college," Dayre admitted.

"You're kidding!" Kenna found herself laughing at the ridiculous coincidence of it all. She was sent to Arnold's Pub to meet one man, and she ended up spending the evening with his college roommate. It was too much!

"What's so funny?" Dayre demanded, his male pride prickling. Was she comparing him to Larry's perfect handsomeness? Did she prefer the suave, debonair approach? God knew Laruda had been popular enough in college, a regular ladies' man.

"I was merely laughing at serendipity," Kenna explained, allaying his worries.

"Serendipity is potent stuff," Dayre countered huskily, brushing a strand of hair away from her forehead. "Nothing to laugh about."

Kenna's breath caught in her throat, as if fearing that the simple reflex of breathing might ruin the moment. Attraction shimmered between them in palpable waves. Ensnared by the lambent passion in his blue eyes, Kenna found herself reveling in the sensual stimulation.

What would it be like, being loved by him? What would it be like to see that lambent passion flaring out of control? Her imagination had just begun to run riot when Dayre surprised her by grabbing her arm.

"Come on," he commanded her. "I guess I owe you lunch and an explanation, in that order!"

This time Kenna allowed herself to be hustled into a nearby restaurant. After placing their orders, they sat back to wait for their food.

"Now that that's out of the way, how about the explanation?" Kenna suggested, her smile tinged with mischief.

Dayre's dark brows lowered, signaling masculine irritation. "You're getting a real kick out of all of this, aren't you?"

"Out of what?" she countered innocently.

"Blowing my cover." The three words were delivered with brisk bluntness.

Kenna was unrepentant. "Your cover deserved to be blown. You really shouldn't stereotype people the way you do. I'm sure the guys on your crew won't think any less of you for being a truthful professor rather than a devious carpenter."

"Is that any way to speak to your luncheon date?" he chastised her, deliberately looking put out.

"It is when that luncheon date doesn't tell me the truth about himself," she retorted. "Why did you feel you had to lie to me?"

"It wasn't actually a lie." Dayre ran an idle hand around the back of his neck, as if easing strained muscles. "I really am a carpenter, you know. I learned the trade while I was still a teenager and used it to supplement my income while I was in college and graduate school. When Harry told me he was shorthanded, I offered to help out until the fall semester begins."

"All right, so your lie was one of omission rather than commission. That still doesn't tell me your motivation."

"In the beginning I was testing," he admitted freely. "I wanted to see what your reaction would be to a carpenter, someone who wouldn't fit in with your political aspirations."

"What reaction were you expecting?" she inquired. "That I'd shudder with distaste and run screaming from the restaurant?"

"Nothing quite that strong," Dayre replied, relieved to see her smile. "It was a spur of the moment reaction on my part. I was shocked to find out that you weren't my blind date—that you were a lady politician."

"What have you got against politicians?" she demanded.

"Nothing personal. I guess you could say I'm suffering from post-Watergate cynicism. But I understand the condition is curable," he added with an appealing grin.

"This test you were giving me," she mocked him. "Did I pass?"

"With flying colors!" he assured her enthusiastically. "I wanted to tell you the truth that first night, but then I kissed you and the thought of everything else went right out of my mind." He paused to bestow a visual caress on her parted lips. "Since then I've been trying to come up with a way to broach the subject. If you recall, when I called you yesterday I did say we had to talk about something."

That was true. Kenna did remember him saying something along those lines.

"Am I forgiven?" he asked with exaggerated penitence.

Deliberating for a moment, she replied, "I'll let you off lightly this time. But next time, Dayre, watch out!"

He winced at her deliberate use of his name. "You're the only one who calls me Dayre."

"So I've heard," she acknowledged with a mocking smile. "I can't imagine why though."

"Can't you?"

"I think it suits you."

Dayre leaned forward, resting his elbows on the table. "Is that so?" His gaze surveyed her face lazily. "What are your plans for tonight?"

She thoughtfully searched her memory. "Tonight I've got an open meeting at one of the local public libraries."

"What about dinner?"

"Dinner is a pot-luck affair with the Hillside PTA."

"Then I envy the Hillside PTA," he stated in a husky growl, "for having a pot-luck affair with you!"

"I'm too old to flirt," she reminded him with a shake of her head.

"That's all right." Under the pretext of patting her hand, his fingers slid between hers. "I'll handle the flirting. You just stick to romantic wrestling and we'll get along fine."

Eyeing their linked hands, she warned him, "The only way we're going to get along is if we're truthful with each other. No more surprises."

Dayre grazed his thumb along the heart of her palm. "Life without surprises is a sure cause of boredom."

"Life with nothing but surprises is a sure cause of ulcers," she retorted sharply, willfully stifling the shivers of awareness threatening her composure.

Dayre heaved a reproachful sigh. "Okay, I'll compromise with you. I'll restrain my surprises to the minor leagues instead of the majors."

"Spoken like a true Met fan, but what constitutes the minor leagues in this instance?"

Dayre raised the fingers of his free hand into the boy scout pledge and vowed, "I'll restrain myself to the telling of tall tales, ma'am."

"So long as the tall tales are no taller than the highest building in Madison," she qualified.

"Seeing as no building is allowed to be taller than the Capitol building, that doesn't give me much leeway!" he complained, his exploring thumb tracing spirals on her palm.

"Giving you too much leeway could be a big mistake," she murmured, slipping her hand from his tempting clasp.

"Or it could be the best thing that ever happened to you. We'll just have to wait and see, won't we?" He paused long enough to gaze at her suggestively before prosaically stating, "I'm starving! How about you?"

Giving him a dose of his own medicine, she replied, "Getting hungrier by the minute!"

The arrival of their waitress precluded Dayre's reply. Setting their sandwiches on the table, she stared at Kenna and then exclaimed, "Hey, you're the lady running for that assembly seat, aren't you?" At Kenna's nod, the waitress continued. "It's a shame what they're doing with the volunteer fire department. My husband's signed up and now the state expects him to . . ." Once started, the waitress went on about her husband's woes until an impatient diner demanded his check.

Dayre picked up his sandwich. "Good thing we didn't order anything that would get cold."

"One of the dangers of eating with a political candidate," she retorted before taking a healthy bite of her sandwich.

Feeling himself watching her with undivided attention, Dayre strove to restrain his thoughts. "The guys said to tell you that you had their vote."

Kenna detected nothing amiss in his voice. "Great!" She dabbed at her mouth with a paper napkin. "I can use all the help I can get."

Hungrily watching her tongue capture a bit of mayonnaise from her upper lip, Dayre was hard pressed to keep his mind on polite conversation. With a concentrated effort he pried his attention away from the tempting moistness of her mouth. "I thought you said things were going well."

"They are, under the circumstances," she qualified.

"What circumstances?"

"There are four other people in this district running for this seat. And that's just within my own party."

"If there are so many people already running, what made you decide to enter the race?"

"I'm the only female candidate."

"Ah!" He nodded knowingly. "So that's the reason."

"Not the only one, no."

"Then what's wrong with the four male candidates?"

"I make it a policy not to tear down my opponents in any race, so I'm not going to go into any heated discussions. All I will say is that I feel I've got the best qualifications for the job."

"A case of the best man for the job being a woman?"

"Exactly."

"How much experience have you had?"

She shot him a reproving look over her tuna on rye. "Enough to know a loaded question when I hear one."

"Well?" he prompted. "What's the loaded answer?"

"Read my campaign brochure," she suggested, her lips curving into a grin.

"Will it tell me what I want to know?"

"Probably not, but it's all you're going to get."

"Oh, I think I'll end up getting a lot more than that, Kenna."

"No doubt you will. You may well end up getting a lot more than you expect. Are *you* busy tonight?"

53

Dayre looked pleasantly startled. "No." Leaning across the Formica table, he asked softly, "What did you have in mind?"

Kenna leaned closer, duplicating his confiding pose. "Making out . . ."

Dayre could hardly believe his luck. "Really?"

". . . voter's registration cards. Part of tonight's program at the library is aimed at increasing voter registration."

"The same way your comment was aimed at increasing my blood pressure?" he asked ruefully.

"I couldn't resist," she acknowledged with a laugh.

"That's what I'm counting on," he added.

The promise of his low voice stayed with her, haunting her thoughts. There was no denying the powerful effect Dayre had on her senses and her emotions. Kenna had not reached the age of thirty-three without her fair share of experience with the opposite sex. But that experience had been more on an equal basis, bordering on platonic, even with the one man she'd been intimate with. She'd never been the sort of woman that men lost their heads over. No, she was more the girl-next-door type, the ones her male friends came to for advice, not passion.

"Well?" Meg and Marilyn demanded in unison the moment she crossed the office threshold. "What happened?"

"I got at least half a dozen promised votes," Kenna returned with her best political smile.

Meg and Marilyn followed Kenna to her office, such as it was. "By your smile I take it that you and Dayre settled things," Meg hazarded to guess.

"I don't think Professor Newport will forget today's luncheon date," Kenna stated, her gaze turning humorously reflective as she recalled the look on Dayre's face when she'd confronted him at the construction site.

"I'm surprised you lived to tell the tale," Marilyn said.

Entering into the spirit of things, Kenna sighed with exaggerated relief. "It was touch and go there for a while."

"Who was touching and where were you going?" Marilyn inquired playfully.

"You're terrible," Kenna reprimanded her, adding the warning, "Someday I'm going to tell Ron."

"He already knows," Marilyn retorted. "I'm terrible and he's impossible. That's why we've stayed married for so long."

"Getting back to Dayre, I'm glad you and he have settled things," Meg said. "I've gotten some feedback from the university and your Professor Newport has some very impressive credentials." Meg referred to her ever-present clipboard. "Age thirty-four, born here in Madison, graduated at the top of his class, written several articles on engineering design, worked on numerous projects around the globe. I could go on and on. The bottom line is that he fits the bill for a political candidate's husband. Why, he's even a registered voter in the right political party—ours!"

Meg's words of commendation didn't please Kenna the way they should have. Instead, she found herself questioning the glowing seal of approval. Kenna had worked hard to get where she was, and she would have to work much harder to win the primary, let alone the election. Was this really the best time to be thinking about personal relationships? Especially one as important as marriage?

Marriage? She caught herself short, verbalizing her thoughts. "What makes you think Dayre is even interested in settling down?"

"The way he looks at you," Meg replied promptly.

"Come on, Meg. I'm no naive nineteen-year-old. That look has nothing to do with matrimony, and everything to do with sexual chemistry."

"The man's thirty-four," Meg replied with unaccustomed defensiveness. "It's high time he was married."

"He may not think so," Kenna pointed out dryly.

"All right. I won't say any more. But should things turn serious, I merely wanted you to know that Dayre does qualify."

"I don't have time for things to turn serious right now," Kenna stated firmly.

Marilyn refused to take her seriously. "I told you I could fit a marriage ceremony in between your meeting with the AAUW and the Meet the Candidate dinner."

"I'm serious. Campaigning is a full-time job, and it leaves little time for eating and sleeping let alone romantic entanglements."

"Depends on how much entangling you do," Marilyn retorted irrepressibly.

"On that note, I think I'll get back to work," Kenna declared. "I've got three pages of questions to answer for the League of Women Voters by the end of the day." The League played an important role in every election, acting as a clearinghouse for information, submitting a list of identical questions to each political candidate. The questions and answers were then printed in a newsletter format available at public libraries or from the League.

Later that evening, Kenna found herself searching the crowd assembled in the public library's meeting room, searching for one man in particular. She hoped he wouldn't wear his Mets cap and faded Levis tonight. This wasn't the crowd for it!

Kenna had exchanged the skirt and checked shirt she'd worn earlier in the day for a less casual two-piece silk dress that was conservative yet stylish. The deep blue material intensified the light blue of her eyes. Her makeup was subtly applied, mascara discreetly darkening her otherwise pale lashes. All in all, the image she projected was one of competence and sympathetic approachability. The latter was extremely important because the object of this open meeting was for the constituents to meet all the candidates, giving the voters an opportunity to voice their concerns and complaints.

The genuine warmth of Kenna's personality made her the most popular of the candidates present. People gathered around her, encouraged by her interest in what they had to say. She'd just shaken what had to be her hundredth hand for the day when her internal antenna told her that Dayre was in the vicinity. Turning her head, she caught sight of him and the sight of him caught at her heart.

Like her, Dayre had dressed appropriately for the meeting. His suit was a conservative gray, his shirt a pale blue, his tie a burgundy silk. He'd avoided appearing overdressed by leaving his suit jacket open, one hand casually tucked into his pants pocket. Kenna had no way of knowing that his hand was actually hidden in his pocket because of his glaringly black and blue thumbnail!

Dayre was soon engaged in conversation with the head librarian and two other men whom Kenna recognized as members of her strongest opponent's campaign staff. She strained to hear what they were talking about, but couldn't pick up a word.

Under other circumstances Kenna would have been very pleased with the chance to make herself known to the voters. As it was, she found it difficult to concentrate, preoccupied as she was with curiosity about Dayre's conversation. By the end of the evening she was worn out from having her attention distracted.

Walking across the now nearly empty parking lot, Kenna inhaled deep breaths of the balmy night air, hoping to clear her mind. A slight wind teased her short blond hair, tossing the carefully cut strands. Opening her car door, she slid her briefcase along the bench-type seat before sliding in after it.

As she inserted her key in the ignition, Dayre persistently remained in her thoughts. He'd left before she could speak to him. Was he angry about her blowing his cover, as he called it? Preoccupied as she was, it took Kenna a moment to realize that her car wasn't starting as it should. In fact, it wasn't starting at all!

The dismal *rrrrr* of the struggling starter muffled the sound of someone rapping on her window. Seeing a dark shadow out of the corner of her eye, Kenna jerked in alarm. The shadow bent down, and Dayre's face was illuminated by the single lamppost in the parking lot.

Relieved, Kenna rolled down her window.

"Having problems?" he inquired with that daredevil grin she was coming to know so well.

"My car won't start." Seeing the knowing glint in his eye, she tacked on decisively, "And before you ask, I filled it with gas this afternoon."

"Try turning it on," he instructed her. After she did so, he listened for a moment before proclaiming, "It sounds like the battery to me. Release the hood."

Kenna groped under the dash for the release handle. Finally finding it, she tugged on it with all her might, but it stubbornly refused to budge. "It's stuck!" she seethed in frustration.

Dayre left his position near the front bumper of the car and came over to the driver's side. Opening the door, he said, "Here, let me try."

The car's interior light provided enough illumination for him to find the handle. It also revealed the fact that the hem on Kenna's silk dress had hiked up, displaying a generous amount of shapely thigh to his appreciative gaze. After one last sidelong glance, Dayre focused his wandering attention on releasing the hood latch. One strong jerk did the trick, not only opening the latch but also propelling his arm backward so that his hand ended up resting on Kenna's lap.

"Sorry about that," he apologized with an unrepentant grin.

"I'll bet you are." She quickly picked up his hand and removed it from her lap. "Can we get on with it, please?"

"Right here in the middle of the parking lot?" Dayre asked with teasing innocence. Catching the reproving look she shot him, he threw his hands up in defense. "All right, all right, I'm going!"

A few minutes later she heard him ask, "Do you have a flashlight, Kenna?"

"I think so." She leaned across to check the contents of the glove compartment. Finding what she was looking for, she answered "Yes," and brought it out to him.

"Shine it over here," he told her.

Kenna held the light steady while Dayre fiddled with the wires leading from the battery. When he finally straightened, his face wore an expression of grim discovery.

"Do you know what's wrong with it?" she asked.

"Either you've had mice nibbling on your cables or else someone's tampered with it." He slammed the hood shut. "Either way, the car's out of commission until we can get it to a garage. I'll give you a lift home, and you can call the motor club from there to come tow your car."

Kenna removed her briefcase and purse from the car before locking it securely. Dayre held open the passenger door to his red Bronco. "Need a leg up?" he asked, indicating the fitted skirt of her dress.

"No thanks, I can manage."

"Too bad," he murmured, watching another generous display of thigh as she attempted to step up into the high cab of the vehicle.

When a slight misjudgment on her part almost resulted in her tumbling onto the blacktopped pavement, Dayre instantly grabbed hold of her, the callused roughness of his hands sure on her waist. "Watch it!"

"You already seem to be doing that," she returned, noting the way his eyes roamed over her limbs.

He rewarded her impudence with a flick from his index finger to the back of her knee. The teasing caress left a trail of fire all the way up her body.

"Let that be a lesson to you," Dayre advised in a professorial tone, closing the passenger door before strolling around to the driver's side.

Kenna watched him hop in behind the wheel, his long-bodied frame moving with ease. Concentrating with an effort, Kenna returned to the subject of her car. "You said that the wires were either eaten by some animal or tampered with?"

"That's right."

"What makes you think they were tampered with?"

"The wires were severed clear through."

"Couldn't a mouse or even a badger do that?"

"They could. Do you normally keep your car in the garage at night?"

"Usually, yes."

"Any problems with mice before?"

"My neighbor has five cats," she replied. "They pretty well keep the neighborhood mouse-free."

"What about other animals?" he prompted. "Badgers, raccoons, oppossums?"

"We've had an occasional raccoon dumping over the garbage cans, but nothing lately."

"The mechanic should be able to give you more details when he looks at it tomorrow."

"You still haven't told me why you suspect foul play."

"You're a political candidate, aren't you. Surely you've heard of dirty tricks?"

"Your post-Watergate cynicism is showing again," she diagnosed.

"I've read *All the President's Men*. I know what kind of things go on." Before she could make a rebuttal, he asked, "Do I turn right or left here?"

"Left." A moment later they pulled up in front of her brick town house and Kenna heard herself inviting him in. "Would you like some coffee?"

"Sounds good," he agreed. Placing a restraining hand on her arm, he ordered her, "Stay put. I'll help you out. Wouldn't want to fall and break your neck, now would you?"

Dayre had no difficulty getting his six-foot-plus frame safely out of the Bronco, jumping down with agile ease. Once he'd opened the passenger door for her, he slid his hands around her waist and lifted her down. Kenna felt as though the formerly solid cement curbing had turned into marshy quicksand beneath her feet. *I must be more tired than I thought,* she rationalized quickly, ignoring the possibility that she was getting in over her head.

After calling the motor club, Kenna switched on the coffeemaker and prepared a tray to bring into the living room. While waiting, Dayre picked up one of her campaign brochures that had been lying on the coffee table.

"This is very impressive," he stated when she brought in the coffee a few minutes later.

"Thank you." She set the tray on the low teak table.

"You have had a lot of political experience," he marveled, looking suitably impressed as he read from the brochure he held in his hand. "From the League of Women Voters right on up to the Planning Commission. And then all these volunteer organizations."

"Come on, you're making me sound like Florence

Nightingale," Kenna protested with a little embarrassment. "I'm not some do-gooder out to cure the world's ills. I think my platform is very down-to-earth, my goals achievable."

"This brochure tells me a lot about Kenna Smith, the candidate, but very little about Kenna Smith, the woman." He exchanged the brochure for the cup of coffee she offered him. "What do you do in your spare time?"

"What spare time?" she countered with a wry grimace, sitting beside him on the wide velour couch.

"I guess that answers my question. Haven't you heard the saying 'All work and no play . . .'?"

"I've heard it, but I don't subscribe to it."

"Ah, a nonbeliever!" Setting his coffee on the table, he asked, "Did I ever tell you about the study my father did on the importance of pleasure in society?"

"No, you didn't," she replied, sipping her coffee. "But I'm sure you're about to remedy that omission."

"In studying various cultures he's found that a society's views of relaxation and pleasure have a direct effect on how productive they are."

Kenna looked on in disbelief. "Really?"

"Would I lie?" he demanded.

In the process of setting her cup on the table, she deliberately drawled, "Well . . ."

"Don't answer that." His hand snaked out to tug her laughing figure into his embrace. "I think a little research might be more productive than mere words."

The kiss began on a teasing note, with whispered assaults on the corner of her mouth. Next came ravishing nibbles, designed to lure her lips apart and invite him inside. The slightly serrated edge of his teeth softly nipped at the lush ripeness of her lower lip until Kenna was forced to return his play. Dayre immediately took advantage of her response. Now that her lips were parted, his tongue entered into the darkened arena, snaring and relinquishing, ambushing and cavorting.

The mutual exploration of their kiss set the tone for what followed. Drawing her closer, Dayre slipped his hands over the evocative silk of her dress. The tips of her shoulders, the ridge of her collarbone, the rounded swell of her breasts, all were subject to the tenderest of seeking caresses.

Kenna's hands did some investigating of their own, sliding under his jacket. There her hands were one layer closer to the hard resilience of his chest. She felt the heat emanating from beneath his smooth cotton shirt, and registered the promise of rippling muscles before she lifted her fingers to loosen his tie. From there it was a mere inch or two to the beckoning angle of his jawline. The slight roughness of his skin provocatively rasped her fingertips. The air carried the message of his tangy aftershave, assailing her senses with a new stimulus.

Dayre's muttered groan was harsh with need. His caressing fingers, which had already begun opening the buttons at the front of her dress, hurriedly finished their task. With an economical movement the fastening of her bra was undone, liberating her breasts and allowing him free access. Kenna felt the tantalizing warmth of his hand upon her, transforming rosy crests into throbbing peaks. Embers of expectancy fanned into uncontrollable flames as his orbiting tongue swirled around the hardened apex, alternately toying and tugging until she was consumed by the velvet warmth of her own desire.

When his lips finally returned to hers, Kenna extended their kiss by clinging to him urgently. The buttons of his shirt were undone by her trembling fingers. Her sighs of pleasure provided the accompaniment to the cleaving of his bare flesh to hers. What had begun as trickling drops of temptation had turned into a raging waterfall of hungry desire. Kenna's dam of self-control was in danger of bursting, letting the swelling torrent of their passion take her where it would.

Warning bells went off in her head, and were soon shrieking in her ear. It was only when Dayre rolled away with a cursed "What the hell!" that she realized the shrieking alarm wasn't only sounding in her head. Something had set off the strident clamor of her smoke alarm!

CHAPTER FIVE

Kenna had to yell in order to be heard over the piercing noise. "I don't believe this!" She stood in the hallway looking up at the blinking alarm with her hands over her ears. "First I have a car that won't start and now I have a smoke alarm that won't quit!"

Dayre stared down at her from his vantage point on top of a chair. He had the cover off the alarm and a moment later had the battery in his hand. "Better?" he inquired, referring to the welcome silence.

"Much."

"Talk about shattering the mood . . ." Dayre ruefully stated, lithely jumping down from the chair.

"What set it off?" Kenna asked, determined to change the subject.

Dayre, however, was equally determined. "Well, now, fiery as things were getting between us, *we* might well have been what set it off."

Kenna refused to be embarrassed. "I doubt that."

"Then would you believe that there's been a recall on this model? You should turn it in and get another one."

Her gaze held an element of suspicion as she asked, "Is that the truth?"

"Would I lie?"

Kenna returned to the living room before answering, "The last time you asked me that question, I ended up getting into trouble." As if reinforcing her statement, she discovered one of her buttons was still undone. Her hands hurriedly attempted to remedy the matter.

"Trouble?" Dayre repeated, brushing her hands aside and replacing them with his own. "Is that what you call it?"

"I think it's a matter of semantics," she retorted, finding it hard to keep her voice steady when her breathing was so irregular.

"And I think we need to discuss the Law of Levels," he stated quietly once her button had been replaced in its buttonhole.

"Is that anything like Murphy's Law?" she quipped, a little unnerved by the seriousness of his expression.

"No. The Law of Levels refers to building—"

"Building?"

"A relationship," Dayre completed. "Basically it says that there are certain levels in a relationship, and that these levels can be speeded up, but they cannot be skipped." His voice turned almost grim. "I think I just skipped a few, and that's why you're backing off."

"I'm not backing off. But I have to say that I'm not in the market for one-night stands," she stated bluntly.

"Neither am I," he returned with equal bluntness.

"Then what are you in the market for?"

Taking his left hand from his pocket, he shoved his fingers through his hair, rumpling the dark strands. "You get right to the point, don't you?"

"So I've been told," she acknowledged absently, her

attention riveted on the bruise coloring his left thumb. "What happened to your hand?"

Startled by the change of subject, Dayre blankly said, "What?"

"Your hand." She tugged his arm down to inspect his injury. "When did you hurt it?"

"This afternoon."

In a flash she remembered the crash of a hammer and the sight of him nursing his left thumb when she'd walked in on him at the construction site. "Oh, Dayre, I'm so sorry." She cradled his hand in hers. "I had no idea you'd hit it so hard. And it was all my fault."

"Don't worry about it. I've felt like I've been hit over the head with a hammer since I first met you!"

With one last regretful touch, Kenna released his hand. "Dayre, I want to be completely honest with you. My free time is going to be extremely limited over the next few months. I don't want to dangle a carrot and keep you waiting for whatever time I may have to spend with you."

"This election is very important to you, isn't it?"

"Very," she agreed. "And I've gone beyond the point of apologizing for being an achiever."

"There's nothing wrong with being an achiever, Kenna."

"There may be nothing wrong with it, but it scares a lot of men."

"I'm not a lot of men," he shot back. "Your intelligence, your ambitions, your drive, are all reasons for admiring you, not being afraid of you!"

Kenna blinked at his vehemence. Dayre took that to be a sign of her exhaustion. It had been a long day for both of them, full of surprises. "I had a long conversation with a few members of Chuck MacCracken's campaign staff tonight," he said. "I meant to bring it up before, but as often happens when I'm with you, I got distracted."

"Is that what you'd call it?" She couldn't resist teasing him.

"Touché," he allowed her. "Anyway, if you want my opinion, I don't think you've got all that much to fear from MacCracken."

"Why do you say that?"

"From the way they were explaining their platform, I think they'll end up hanging themselves from it."

Kenna thought the same thing, but she hadn't expected Dayre to be equally observant. Before she could comment, he went on to say, "It's getting late and you look beat."

"I am beat," she admitted, "and I've still got a pile of papers to go through by tomorrow morning's strategy meeting."

"Then get to bed." He dropped a quick kiss on the lips she'd delicately parted in a yawn. Adding a nibbling caress to her ear, he whispered, "Alone, for the time being!" One last potent kiss, and then he was gone.

Dayre remained in her thoughts long afterward. The image of his face came between her and the statistics on the printed pages she was studying. The memory of his touch was woven into her dreams, coloring them with climactic passion.

Early the next morning Kenna had to cadge a lift from Marilyn, who lived only a few blocks away. The garage had promised that they'd have Kenna's car finished by the end of the day.

"What broke?" Marilyn asked as they drove to the campaign office.

"Dayre thought the wires from the battery had been cut."

"Cut? I don't like the sound of that."

"Now you're beginning to sound like Dayre. The wires were probably gnawed by a hungry mouse or a badger."

"I certainly hope that's the case," Marilyn murmured, parking her car in front of the storefront office.

The fate of Kenna's sedan was forgotten once the strategy meeting began. The discussion centered on analyzing the opposition.

"I think we'll find that the strongest runner of the four other candidates will be Charles 'Chuck' Mac-Cracken," Meg stated, referring to her ever-present clipboard. "According to the financial report he filed, he's got the most money behind him."

"What about Dave Frobisher?" Kenna asked. She and Dave had worked together on efforts to reform the school district funding.

"Dave's a good man," Meg admitted. "I know you had some doubts when you heard you would be running against him. But look at it this way. Things could be worse. Had the incumbent not decided to retire, none of you would be running!"

"Are you trying to tell me the more, the merrier?" Kenna mocked.

"I'm saying that the five-way split of the vote may well be to our advantage. I think the other four male candidates will split the traditional party vote, while you'll be picking up a lot of independent support as well as the women's vote."

Kenna nodded in agreement before pointing out, "You haven't mentioned anything about Buzz Gordon or John Dickson."

Meg ticked them off derisively. "Dickson doesn't have any political experience whatsoever, and the state assembly is no place to get on-the-job training. I think it's presumptuous of him, to say the least, to be running in this race at all. Buzz Gordon is a terrible public speaker and his organization isn't very cohesive. He hasn't said a thing about his goals for the district; all he's done is try to badmouth the opposition. No, I think of the four, MacCracken and Frobisher are the ones we have to beat."

"Our latest telephone canvass shows that you're gaining support in the western sections of the district," Marilyn offered.

Kenna sipped at her cup of lukewarm coffee. "That's the area where I made all those public appearances, right?"

"Right. I've set up a similar schedule in the eastern, southern, and northern sections as well." Part of Marilyn's duties were to ensure that Kenna put in appearances in every part of the district.

"What about that newspaper interview?" Kenna asked.

"That's set for tomorrow," Marilyn answered. "There are also several radio spots that I've set up for you. And then there's the big do on public TV right before the primary."

The next several weeks were so busy that Kenna didn't even have the time to change her scenic wall calendar from June to July. To begin with, the mechanic was unable to ascertain the cause of the car's

71

severed wires. "They might have been cut," he admitted lackadaisically. "But I couldn't swear to it." Then there was the Fourth of July four-day weekend and all its accompanying nonstop stumping. The highlight of that hectic time was receiving her first official endorsement from the National Organization for Women with an accompanying donation to her needy campaign fund.

As she'd predicted, her time with Dayre was extremely limited. In fact, although he did phone her at least once a day without fail, she hadn't spent any time alone with him since that night the smoke alarm had gone off. For that reason she made it a point to set aside an entire Sunday in late July for a picnic with Dayre. The date was arranged weeks in advance, which might have explained why that particular Sunday was the only rainy day they'd had so far during the entire month!

"Murphy's Law," Kenna claimed with a disgusted look out the rain-smeared windshield of Dayre's Bronco.

Dayre turned the wipers onto high before stating, "Nothing is going to spoil our day together."

"How can we have a picnic in this downpour?"

"Easy. We simply move our picnic inside."

"Inside?"

"That's right," he confirmed. "Inside my apartment."

Kenna had to admit to a certain curiosity about the place where he lived. She'd always found that a man's surroundings told a lot about him. Dayre's apartment was no exception. Located near the sprawling University of Wisconsin campus, it was a third floor walk-up in one of a block of houses converted for university housing.

"It's close to work," Dayre said by way of excusing the lack of glamor. "In good weather I'll be able to bike to work."

The apartment's interior was as unique as the exterior was staid. One wall was taken up with do-it-yourself bookshelves made out of bricks and pine planking and filled with hardcover texts. A well-worn couch was offset by a huge cedar table, the natural beauty of the wood making it a showpiece. A one-of-a-kind pyramid-shaped storage unit held a compact stereo, a large cassette collection, and a wide assortment of geodes.

"What do you think?" Dayre asked, ushering her inside and helping her off with her raincoat.

Her response was concise but appreciative, an unwitting echo of his opinion of her place. "It's you." Strolling over for a closer look, she asked, "Did you make this cabinet yourself?"

Dayre nodded. "That, the bookcases, and the tables."

"I'm impressed!" She toured the room leisurely, appreciating the numerous curios he had displayed here and there. "Where did you get this?" She held up a unique wood carving.

"Tahiti," he replied.

Holding up another object, she asked, "What's this?"

His grin should have warned her. "A Hindu fertility god."

"Figures," she muttered, cautiously replacing the statue. Moving on to the L-shaped corner windows, she was almost afraid to ask, "How about these?" She indicated two metal loops fastened onto the woodwork.

"I'll show you later. First, let's eat." With that he took the plaid blanket that was folded over one end of the couch and spread it out on the hardwood floor of the living room. With an inviting sweep of his hand, he announced, "Madame's table is ready!"

"I'm not sure I'm dressed for such an elegant establishment," Kenna teased.

Dayre's appreciative gaze ran over the navy blue shirt and beige slacks she was wearing. "You look good enough to eat."

"Thank you, kind sir." Accepting his helping hand, she agilely settled onto the blanket. "Now, what've you got in the basket?" He'd had the wicker basket with him since he'd picked her up.

"Patience, my dear."

"I'm starving!" she complained.

"Good!"

"You won't think so when my stomach starts growling," she warned. "It will echo around the room."

"I was just practicing another theory I heard."

"What's that?" She made a move to sneak around him and got caught with her hand in the picnic basket. "Starve your guests and they'll do anything?"

"Close." Lifting her captured hand to his lips, he kissed it with Continental flare. "The way to a woman's heart is through her stomach."

"Sounds like a painful operation to me," she teased him.

Releasing her hand, Dayre groaned and handed her a plate. "Here, eat your chicken."

"This is delicious!" she complimented him. "It tastes as good as Marilyn's recipe."

"That's probably because it is her recipe," Dayre relayed.

"You mean that *you* made this?" She waved a drumstick in incredulous astonishment.

"Of course. And get that chauvinistic look off your face," he reprimanded her. "There's no reason a man can't cook as well as a woman. In fact, my mother insisted that both my sister and myself know how to cook. She didn't want either one of us drifting into marriage because of a lack of decent nourishment!"

"What else did your mother teach you?"

"I can sew on a mean button and do my own laundry and ironing."

"Then I'm surprised some woman hasn't snatched you up."

"I don't respond well to snatching," Dayre replied with all the primness of a Victorian miss.

Kenna laughed at the absurdity of his deliberately high-pitched voice paired with the unquestionable virility of his physique. His thin baseball jersey, with the word *Mets* emblazoned on the front, molded his broad shoulders like a second skin. His tan had darkened over the past few weeks, and the dark bronze accentuated the blue blaze of his eyes.

"I can see that you're the type of man that would want a woman's respect," Kenna acknowledged dutifully.

"Absolutely. I allow only respectful snatching. Like this." He demonstrated by swooping down and snatching a kiss. His mouth was there and gone before Kenna could respond.

Nonchalantly picking up another piece of chicken, she asked, "Do you really do all your own laundry and all those other domestic things?"

"Would I lie?"

"Oh, no, you don't." She shook her head, laughing. "I got caught on that question last time."

Dayre's answering laughter showed his appreciation of her humor. After polishing off the last of the chicken, he explained, "I found that it was necessary to be self-sufficient while traveling. When I worked in Africa, there weren't any volunteers lined up to do my wash, and the canteen food was pretty bad."

"You worked in Africa?" Kenna tossed her clean-picked bones onto the paper plate supplied for that purpose.

"Building dams," he clarified. "Didn't I tell you?"

"No."

"Then this is the time to bring out the surprise."

"What surprise?" She wiped her greasy hands on the damp wipe he handed her.

"Stay here a minute and you'll find out."

Dayre returned a few moments later, carrying what looked to be a handful of rope.

"After feeding your guests, you tie them up?" Kenna asked, teasing.

"What a lurid imagination you have! We'll have to discuss that sometime. Right now I've got something to show you." He headed for the corner windows and hooked one end of the pile of rope onto the loop. When the other end was hooked onto the opposite loop Kenna realized the rope was actually a hammock.

"We used these in Africa, you know," he informed

her. "It was safer sleeping this way. No chance of creepy crawlies climbing the bedpost."

"Doesn't sound like my cup of tea." Kenna shuddered.

"It was so exciting, lying there listening to the chatter of the chimps, the occasional roar of a lion on the prowl. In fact, there was one occasion when a man-eating lion got into the compound."

Imagining the danger of his sun-warmed body being mauled by vicious teeth made her voice unsteady. "What happened?"

"I was sleeping in my hammock, dead to the world."

When he paused, lost in memories, Kenna impatiently prodded, "Well?"

"First I heard a rustle near the door."

"And then?"

"I felt heavy breathing on my face."

"The lion?" she breathed in fear.

Dayre solemnly nodded, adding, "I swear they could hear me all the way to Brazilia."

"Brazilia?" Kenna repeated, suddenly suspicious. "Brazilia is in South America, not Africa."

The grin on his face said it all.

"You fake!" Had there been a pillow handy, she would have thrown it at him. "You were spinning a line the whole time, weren't you?"

Dayre didn't answer her accusation. Instead he invited her to try the hammock. "Come on, try it and you'll know what I'm talking about."

Kenna shook her head. "Unh-unh. It'll probably collapse the minute I sit on it!"

"Nonsense. Here, I'll show you."

And so he did, kicking off his running shoes to sit on the hanging bed. Gripping the sides with a sure hold, he swung his feet up and a moment later was lying supine, hands clasped behind his head. "See, it's easy."

"Sure it is."

"If you won't come here, then I'll have to come get you," he warned her.

"You wouldn't dare."

It was the wrong thing for her to say, because a moment later he leapt from the hammock. Kenna watched with widened eyes as he tugged the baseball jersey over his head and tossed it into a corner. Blue eyes glinting with devilish humor, he pounded his fists on his now bare chest and gave a fair impersonation of Tarzan's famous cry.

Kenna scrambled to her feet, laughter slowing her retreat.

Dayre had no difficulty catching her, and he had no difficulty swinging her up into his arms and triumphantly carrying her to the hammock.

"Me, Tarzan, you, Jane," he growled, efficiently dumping her onto the roped bed.

Kenna had one hand gripping the side of the hammock and the other gripping her own side, where laughter was threatening to give her a stitch.

Dayre's hands soon replaced hers as he joined her on the hammock.

"I don't think there's room for two in here!" She panicked, scrambling off the other side and almost tumbling them both onto the floor. As it was, Dayre made a grab to catch her, but the only thing that ended up getting caught was his silver belt buckle, which was securely hooked by the hemp twine of the rope hammock!

Kenna snuck a look over her shoulder, surprised that Dayre hadn't followed in hot pursuit.

"Did you plan this?" he demanded, glaring down at the offending belt buckle.

"Surely a jungle guide like yourself would know better than to wear a belt buckle into a hammock," Kenna stated.

"Cute, real cute. Come help me."

"Why, D.J.," she cooed. "I thought you didn't like girls who snatched!"

His only reply was a threatening growl that fit in well with the jungle ambience he'd already created. Another attempt on his part to release the buckle served only to tangle it twice as much.

Seeing the bigger mess he was making of it, she relented and said, "All right, I'll help you."

"So I should hope. After all, it's your fault that I'm in this predicament."

"My fault?"

"If you hadn't gone leaping away, I wouldn't have had to chase after you."

"As I recall, you never got around to the chasing part," she couldn't resist pointing out.

"Come closer, little girl," he growled.

"Umm, how should we go about doing this?" she asked, cautiously moving forward to survey the situation.

Dayre's exaggerated plea of "Very carefully" won him a jab in the ribs.

"You're enjoying this, aren't you?" she accused him.

"I'm making the best of a touchy situation," he maintained stoically.

"Maybe I should get out the rope and tie you up," she threatened.

"Kenna, you shock me! I had no idea you went in for that sort of thing."

"I don't. Keep quiet and let me concentrate."

"Yes, ma'am," he answered with mocking obedience.

"Maybe I should just get a knife and cut you loose," she mused.

Dayre's hand shot out to manacle her wrist. "Forget it! I think, between us, we should be able to manage freeing me."

Kneeling on the floor beside him, Kenna set to work, her fingers nimbly laboring to free him. She could hear the increasing unsteadiness of his breathing as she came into unavoidable contact with the most sensitive part of his anatomy. "Sorry," she murmured as her touch gave rise to his desire, an occurrence the taut denim of his jeans did little to disguise.

"You sure you're not trying to torture me?" he demanded huskily.

"That was an accident," she defended herself. "This"—her fingers slid a little lower—"is torture!"

"Ah, but what sweet torture!" His voice was raspy with desire.

With perfect timing Kenna managed to finally free the buckle. A moment later Dayre had flipped it open and slid the leather belt from his waist. With one hand he tossed the troublesome belt to the floor while the other tugged her into his embrace. Sprawled atop him, Kenna found herself trapped.

Dayre discarded the preliminaries. His mouth fastened on hers, hungry in its intent. Her lips were parted and eagerly returned the measure of his desire. Ravishing kisses deepened with each encounter, and playfulness gave way to urgency. Each gave to the other, both sharing in the ultimate rewards.

The bare warmth of Dayre's chest invited her exploration. Her admiring fingers slid along his side, climbing the curve of his ribs from waist to arm. Touching him was like striking a match—the end result was a thermal flare that dissolved her restraints. Melting into him, she curved her arms around his waist to his back, fingertips coming together to rest on the indentation of his spine. Kenna gave no thought to the fact that her unfettered passion amounted to wanton invitation. All she could think of was how strong he was, how good he felt.

Kenna's eager response further stimulated Dayre's already painfully heightened needs. Her silken arms and seeking lips almost drove him over the edge. Striving to slow down the headlong pace of their lovemaking, he set a new, slower rhythm. Lips that had formerly engulfed hers lifted to bestow delicious nibbles and caresses. His hands lazily tugged her shirttail from her pants, trailing beneath the material with long hypnotic strokes.

The slower pace of their lovemaking prolonged their pleasure, and suspended time. But even so, when her legs entangled themselves with his, the firm tautness of the muscles in his thighs indicated the volatility of his desire.

Regaining some portion of her common sense, Kenna leaned away to murmur, "We're going to get into trouble if we don't stop this soon." Her warning was rendered practically useless by the string of tiny kisses she attached to it.

"I know." Dayre's muttered acknowledgment was equally futile as his lips traced the curve of her face.

Her hand slid across his jaw, loving the five o'clock roughness of his skin. "We should stop."

"Kenna . . ."

"Hmmm?"

"Marry me!"

CHAPTER SIX

Kenna's voice was shaking as she asked, "What did you say?"

"You heard me. I said, marry me."

"You can't be serious." She drew far enough away from him to study his expression.

"Even I draw the line at making false marriage proposals," Dayre drawled, easily subduing her attempts to free herself.

Momentarily acknowledging defeat, Kenna temporarily abandoned her struggles. "You can't propose to someone you've only known a month," she protested.

"Actually it's been four weeks and five days," he corrected her, combing his fingers through her hair.

"But during that time we've seen each other only a couple of times. You can't seriously think we know each other well enough for marriage!"

"Sure I can." Noting her mutinous expression, he released her with a sigh. "I can see this discussion is going to get serious. Maybe we should retire to a less provocative locale," he suggested with a degree of levity, noting their continued proximity in the hammock.

She scrambled to her feet with more speed than grace.

Dayre followed suit, his voice halting her retreat. "Kenna, I'm thirty-four. I've been around enough to know that you're the woman I want to spend the rest of my life with. If your only reservation is that we haven't known each other long enough, then I'll simply wait and ask you again. Say, in a week."

"A week?" Kenna didn't know whether to laugh or cry.

"You're right." Sensing her indecision, he applied a dose of humor. "That's too long! I'll ask you every day until you say yes. I don't handle rejection very well, you see," he explained modestly.

"I'm getting that impression," she acknowledged wryly.

"So what do you say?"

"I don't know what to say." She shook her head in an effort to clear her thoughts. "I'm finding it hard to accept that you're serious about this."

"Why's that?"

Kenna hated having to put it into words, so she kept her explanation brief. "Because we both know I'm not the type of woman that men lose their heads over."

Dayre's eyes narrowed, guarding his expression from her. "You're not?"

"Of course not," she retorted. "I'm the clean-cut older-sister type."

Realizing she was actually serious, he shook his head in utter amazement. "Where did you get an idea like that?"

"From the past thirty-three years of my life."

"You can't mean that no one has proposed marriage to you before."

His masculine incredulity should have boosted her

morale, but it didn't. "No, I don't mean that." Her voice came close to bitterness as she went on. "I seem to be blessed with the type of looks and personality that men want to take home to present to their mothers."

"Did you accept any of those proposals?"

"One."

Knowing Kenna was now single, Dayre had never thought to ask her if she'd been married before. "You married him?"

"No. Luckily I realized I was making a mistake before any permanent damage was done." That was the closest thing to a lie Kenna had ever told Dayre, for damage had been done.

"What about the other proposals?"

Kenna shrugged. "They never felt right."

"And does it feel right with me?" Dayre growled in a deep voice.

"I'm not denying that there's a chemistry between us," she replied candidly. "There has been from the first time I saw you at Arnold's Pub. But don't you see that chemistry is not a stable enough foundation for marriage?"

He reached out a hand to smooth the earnest expression from her face. "Then how about love? Is that stable enough?"

"Love?" Kenna repeated, shaken by this new turn of events.

"Surely you don't think I'd ask you to marry me if I didn't love you?"

Feeling the familiar tug of attraction, she whispered, "I don't know what to think."

"Then don't think at all," he advised her, his warm gaze inviting her into his arms. "Just feel."

"No." Kenna broke free. "I'm not the type to be swept off my feet by emotion!" Her fierce words were for her own benefit as much as Dayre's. "I won't let that happen. I've worked too hard to get where I am."

"I hardly expect you to quit the campaign and settle down as a *hausfrau,*" Dayre protested. "I'm very proud of what you've accomplished in the course of your career, both as a teacher and as a public official. I think you've got a lot to offer this state as a representative and I would never dream of interfering with your dreams."

"What's in this marriage for you?" she demanded bluntly.

"The answer's simple—you!" He raised a hand to silence Kenna's words of protest. "No, let me finish. You say that you're not the type of woman to knock a man off his feet?"

"Actually, the way I put it was 'make a man lose his head,' " she corrected him.

"Whatever. Now, I can't speak for the men you've known in the past; I can only speak for myself. And as far as I'm concerned, you're more than enough woman for me."

How could she tell him that the burn she'd received from her broken engagement eight years ago had left scars that even now affected her. She'd thought that George had wanted her for herself, that finally passion had come into her life. But that fantasy had lasted only until she'd overheard him talking to a group of his friends at a cocktail party. There George had gone into detail about how unsatisfactory Kenna had been in bed, and how he'd sought supplemental loving from other women. When asked why he bothered with Kenna, George's reply had been that none of the other women were the type you could "take home."

That experience was the reason Kenna had agreed to go along with Meg's plan to find her a husband, one that would fit in with her political aspirations. After all, men had been doing it for years, marrying for reasons of expediency. Here was Kenna's chance to get even.

But Kenna found that she didn't want to get even at Dayre's expense. Emotions weren't supposed to have played a part in the final decision. Yet something within her had backed off of the plan. She'd found fault with all the prospective marital candidates, all except Dayre, who was never intended to be a candidate in the first place.

Dayre's hand tenderly caressing the curve of her cheek brought her back from the past. "Where were you?"

Her eyes were shadowed with memories. "I was thinking."

"You were a million miles away." He entwined his fingers with hers. "Listen, Kenna, I realize you're under a lot of pressure right now, with the primary only a little over a month away. I certainly don't want to create any more stress for you, so don't go off in any meditative trances on me, okay? Just know that I love you, and that things will work out fine. When we're old and gray and married you'll look back on this time with fondness. It'll be something to tell the grandkids, how their grandmother had a hard time accepting their grandfather's proposal of marriage."

"You like kids?"

"I grew up with them," Dayre replied with a glint of humor.

"Are you hoping for a large family?"

"I'm hoping to have you as my wife. Anything above and beyond that is icing on the cake."

Kenna frowned at his words. "What about an heir to carry on the Newport family name?"

"I don't happen to think that's a good enough reason to have children. Parenting is a serious job, requiring a lot of time and effort for it to be done properly."

"I agree."

"How about you?" he questioned her. "How do you feel about kids?"

"I'm not really sure," Kenna admitted with due honesty. "I'm thirty-three; that's fairly old to be starting a family."

"More and more women are delaying pregnancy until they're settled in a career. If you wanted, there's nothing to say that we couldn't have a child after you'd settled into your role as a state assemblywoman. The capitol is only an hour away from here, so you wouldn't have the long commuting problem that some other legislators might have."

"You sound very convincing."

"That's because I intend to marry you, lady, come hell or high water!"

It's the hell I'm afraid of, Kenna returned silently. Aloud, she murmured, "I wish I could be so sure."

"You will be." He dropped a decisive kiss on the tip of her nose. "And I'll wait until you are."

His words, meant to reassure her, did anything but that. Despite Kenna's competence and self-confidence in the public eye, she now found herself at a loss. Her emotions and reservations were a mass of tangled ties —ties to the past and to the future.

Knowing she had to talk to someone or go crazy, Kenna chose Marilyn as her confidante. She phoned her later that evening and got right to the point. "Marilyn, I need your advice. Dayre's asked me to marry him."

"Great!" Marilyn enthused. "Congratulations! When's the big day?"

"You don't understand." Kenna kicked off her shoes and made herself comfortable; this was likely to be a long call. "I didn't say yes."

Marilyn's tone was frankly disbelieving. "You turned him down?"

"No. I said I needed more time."

"Why?"

"Oh, Marilyn, it's so complicated."

"In that case give me the bottom line," her friend suggested.

"I guess the bottom line is that I'm not sure Dayre loves me."

"Hasn't he said?"

"Yes." Kenna's fingers worried the coiled phone wire. "He says he loves me, but I'm not sure I believe him."

Disbelief had turned to confusion. "Why should Dayre lie about something like this?"

"It's not a case of lying," Kenna stalled.

"Then what is it a case of?"

"I think I may just be a new experience for Dayre Newport. I mean, I walk up to him in a pub and claim him for dinner. I walk up to him in the middle of his construction crew and blow his cover. Maybe he's just infatuated."

"You're not making any sense. What you did sounds more like grounds for divorce than infatuation!"

"I never claimed that I'd make sense," Kenna flared out, frustrated by her own inability to express herself. "I'm sorry, I didn't mean to snap at you," she apologized on a quieter note.

"That's all right. What are friends for if you can't abuse them?" Marilyn inquired cheerfully. "But getting back to Dayre, why do you find it hard to believe that he loves you?"

"Marilyn, you've known me for how long now?"

Marilyn paused a minute to do her addition. "Must be ten years now."

"And in all that time, have you ever known me to knock a man's eyes out?"

"You've been ready to knock a few blocks off, but no, I can't recall you blinding anyone."

"Exactly."

"Exactly what?"

"I'm not the type of woman to inspire that kind of passion in a man."

"That's one way of looking at it, I suppose." Kenna was actually disappointed to hear Marilyn agreeing with her. "Of course," Marilyn went on to say, "the other way of looking at it is to concentrate on the type of man you've associated with. Ever since you broke your engagement with George, you've been sticking with a certain type of man."

"And what type of man is that?"

"The type who compartmentalizes women into two

groups—those you go to bed with and those you take home to mother."

Kenna winced at Marilyn's phraseology.

"But, Kenna, there are other men who don't suffer from Madonna complexes. Men like Dayre."

"But this isn't the right time to fall in love!" Kenna's protest came out as a soft wail. "I don't have time for it now. The primary is only a few weeks away!"

"I've always maintained that it's not the quantity of time you spend with someone, but the quality. It seems to me that in the short time you and Dayre have had together you've come to know each other fairly well. Am I right?"

Kenna assented. "You're right."

"When you first met him you were in seventh heaven. Your exact words were 'I've found Mr. Right!' At least that's what Meg claims."

"Meg's right."

"Then what went wrong?"

"Nothing went wrong exactly. It was more a gradual awakening to reality."

"And what's the reality?"

"That as a candidate I'm going to be spending almost every waking moment campaigning from now until the primary. And after that is another seven weeks of campaigning for the November election. If I win, there's all the work involved with being a legislator."

"I never claimed it would be easy, Kenna. But then it wasn't easy initiating team teaching at your school, or being the first woman on the planning commission."

"I must be a masochist," Kenna decided wryly.

91

"Let me close on a note of caution. Don't throw away your chance of happiness because the timing is inconvenient. If Dayre is willing to wait, then make the most of it. There! That's all the advice this married lady of twenty-one years is going to give."

Kenna had barely hung up the phone when it rang again.

"Well?" Dayre began without bothering with a greeting. "Did you talk to your friends about me?"

"We had a conference call," Kenna teased him.

"And? Did they tell you to dump me?"

"No, quite the opposite, as a matter of fact."

"Ah! They recognize my inherent good qualities."

"And your acceptability as a candidate's fiancé."

"Then as far as I can see, you're the only one with reservations about this. Majority rule means you're outnumbered."

"I'm still tallying the votes," she stalled.

"Tally or dally all you like, Kenna." His deep voice stroked its way to her heart. "I have every intention of winning in the end."

By early the next morning Kenna was once again in the midst of heavy campaigning. Meg's latest telephone canvass showed that Kenna, MacCracken, and Frobisher were running neck in neck. The slew of appearances Kenna was making all across the district had resulted in the increased recognition of her by name. At the Meet the Candidate functions, her warm smile and informatively succinct speaking style added to her growing popularity.

After a long day and evening fulfilling political obligations, Kenna came to depend on Dayre's nocturnal phone calls. He'd kept his promise to propose to her every day, often popping the question in the middle of a casual conversation. "The Mets won today, will you marry me?"

"Someday I'm going to say yes," Kenna warned him, "and then you won't know what to do."

"Oh, I'll know what to do all right." Dayre's voice held the promise of intimacy. "Don't worry about that."

After another ten days of heavy campaigning, Kenna was ready for a break. She hadn't had a day off since her indoor picnic with Dayre. When a day-long seminar she'd been scheduled to attend was unexpectedly canceled at the last minute, she phoned Dayre with the good news.

"Guess what?" she demanded eagerly.

"What?"

"Guess."

"You won the state lottery."

"Wisconsin doesn't have a state lottery. Guess again."

"All the other contenders in the primary have withdrawn from the race, knowing that you are by far the best candidate."

"No such luck," Kenna sighed. "But I do have a free day tomorrow."

"A free day!" Dayre's voice held deliberate astonishment. "That's better than winning the lottery. I'll pick you up at nine thirty and let you sleep late for a change. Dress casually."

"Wait a minute. Where are we going?"

"We're going to play tourist for the day."

"Is that anything like playing doctor?" she asked.

93

"It could be arranged," he warned. "Just be ready at nine thirty."

"You call that casual?" Dayre demanded as she let him in the next morning.

"What's wrong with it?" she questioned, smoothing her hands down the pale blue cotton of her military-type jumpsuit.

Dayre circled her, saying, "It lacks something. Ah-ha!" He snapped his fingers. "I've figured it out. This is what it needs." He tugged his red Mets cap off his head and placed it on top of hers. "There! That's much better. Now all you need are these." He whipped out a pair of oversized sunglasses that made Kenna crack up. "Don't laugh," he rebuked. "I almost bought you a pair that glow in the dark!"

"Why not a pair of the skinny ones some of my teenage students seem to favor?"

"The punk look," Dayre identified. "Those were all sold out."

"Lucky for me," she murmured, modeling the glasses. "Think anyone would recognize me?" She struck a theatrical pose.

"Not a chance. The Mets cap does the trick. Do you have your camera?"

"Right here. Why?"

"We're going to be visiting your future place of employment, so we want to be sure and take lots of pictures." Dayre was already hustling her out the door.

"Future place of employment? You don't mean
. . ."

". . . the capitol building. When was the last time

94

you went on a tour of your state's impressive marble edifice?"

"A tour? Not since I was in college," Kenna admitted, quickly adding, "I've been there since for committee meetings—"

"That's all well and good," Dayre interrupted her, "but today we're going there as tourists." Flamboyantly rearranging the red bandanna he wore around his neck, he introduced himself as "Joe Smuthers from Eureka, Kansas. And you're my wife, Flo."

The legislature was not in session during the summer, so Kenna had no fear of running into someone she knew. A guided tour had just started when they arrived in the domed building's lobby. "Run and you can catch up with it," the information clerk told them.

Dayre took the woman's advice literally, bolting up the stairs with a speed that left Kenna breathless. "Next time you decide to try out for the hundred-yard dash, remember to let go of my hand," she huffed, more short-winded than angry.

"I'm not letting go of you ever," he returned, linking his fingers more tightly through hers.

"That might make eating rather difficult," she pointed out as they joined the group of tourists.

"But think what you could do with an extra pair of hands in the shower," he said, sotto voce.

The image he evoked was responsible for her missing the first segment of their tour guide's memorized spiel.

"Pay attention, dear," Dayre instructed Kenna with husbandly affection. "There'll be a test afterward."

"Oh, goody!" she purred. "I do so enjoy your pop quizzes."

The crowd turned around to stare at the man in blue jeans who seemed to be choking.

"The State Capitol was designed by George Post in 1906," the guide stated, calling the group's attention to her. "The construction took about ten years to complete at a cost of a little over seven million dollars. The exterior is made of blocks of Bethel Vermont granite while the interior building materials include many fine pieces of marble and granite imported from as far away as Norway and Algiers. If you'll follow me, we'll head for the Assembly Chambers."

Once inside the chambers, Kenna's attention again drifted away from the guide's voice. Instead, her mind was filled with visions of her sitting in one of these heavy chairs, debating the issues with other legislators and casting her vote on the computerized tallyboard with its green and red lights.

"Stand there, dear, I want to take your picture," Dayre said as the other members of the tour trooped onward. "Where are you going?" he demanded as she walked toward the far side of the room.

"This will be my seat when I win the election," she stated, stopping behind one of the dark green magisterial chairs.

He took the picture and a minute later, thanks to the miracles of instant photography, they both viewed the photograph of a tall woman wearing a jumpsuit and a baseball cap. "I think this would make a great publicity photo for you. I can see the caption now. A WOMAN'S PLACE IS IN THE HOUSE."

"And the Senate," Kenna quickly tacked on.

They caught up with the tour group as they walked around the rotunda. "The height of the State Capitol building from the esplanade to the top of the statue on the dome is 285.9 feet," the guide was saying. "It was intentionally designed to be seven inches shorter than the U.S. Capitol in Washington. Normally we would continue the tour with the Senate chambers, but they're being repainted this afternoon. Since the Supreme Court is in special session today, I'm afraid this ends our tour for today."

"I guess you'll have to wait until you're elected to get the full tour," Dayre told Kenna. His inflection resembled a mocking grumble as he said, "I can't believe our luck in having both the Senate chambers and the Supreme Court taken off the itinerary."

"Let's go drown our sorrows in a banana split," Kenna suggested.

"A banana split?"

"Sure. Made with some of that famous ice cream from U. of W.'s Babcock Hall."

A half hour later Dayre and Kenna sat down on a pair of white wrought iron chairs in an old-fashioned ice cream parlor near the university. "I would never have expected someone as conservative as yourself to order cinnamon, malted milk, and peanut butter–flavored ice cream," he said.

"I am not conservative," Kenna objected.

"When a jumpsuit is your idea of casual, you're conservative."

"I'll have you know that I'm known as a moderate. Besides, your choice of French vanilla, German chocolate, and English toffee is hardly sedate. You know what they say about people in glass houses."

"You don't understand," he professorially dismissed

97

her criticism. "French, German, and English flavors reflect my status as a world traveler."

Their high-spirited banter continued through the late afternoon and evening as they strolled across the university campus, considered one of the most beautiful in the country. "The trees will be changing soon," Kenna noted.

"Classes will be starting soon, the end of next week to be precise."

Kenna knew, without his saying it, that the beginning of classes would cut even more into their already limited time together. Was this any way to conduct a relationship, grabbing a few hours here or there? It was certainly no way to start a marriage. Was it?

I'm not going to let my misgivings ruin today, she said to herself with determination. "Where shall we go for dinner?" she asked.

"I've got somewhere special in mind," he drawled, heading back to the lot where he'd parked the Bronco.

"Your place?"

"No. Arnold's Pub. Don't you know what day this is?"

"It's Monday, August thirteenth."

"That's right, and . . . ?"

"And?" she repeated blankly.

"And what's special about that date?"

"I give up."

"You give up! That proves it."

"Proves what?"

"Men are more romantic than women."

Romantic? Arnold's Pub? The date? Ah-ha! "Just because I did not immediately recall that today is our eight-week anniversary, you should not assume that I'm less romantic than you are."

"I'm the one who's got to have broken a record for the number of marriage proposals I've made. At least to the same woman," he amended.

"How many times has it been now?" she asked with deliberate vagueness, although she already knew the exact number.

"Twenty-two times!"

"Not counting today," she added, thereby letting him know that she remembered each and every one of the proposals.

"So you are paying attention," he noted in amusement. "I was beginning to wonder."

They'd reached the parked Bronco by now.

While waiting for him to unlock the passenger door for her, she archly retorted, "I always pay attention."

"How encouraging!" He dropped a quick kiss on her parted lips. "Should I also take heart from the fact that you're wearing my baseball cap? Does this mean we're going steady?"

"Do I get to keep the cap if I say no?"

Dayre shook his head. "It's a package deal."

"In that case I guess we're going steady. I couldn't bear to part with this cap now that I've gotten accustomed to it."

"Listen, lady, you're pressing your luck." He added a reprimanding flick to the visor of the Mets cap. "Any more of this disrespect and I won't buy you dinner."

Arnold's Pub was as busy as it had been that first night they'd met. Luckily the restaurant's informal decor allowed for casual dress, but Kenna did remove the baseball cap and sunglasses once they were seated in a secluded booth.

"This is much cozier than the table we were given last time we were here," Dayre decided, nudging his knee against hers.

"Stop that!" She reached under the table to deliver a playful slap to his knee.

"You two ready to order now?" another voice intruded to ask.

Kenna and Dayre looked at each other in disbelief. It was the same waiter who had hurried them out last time.

"We'll have the garden basket appetizers to start and then two sirloin steaks, one rare and one medium," Dayre ordered promptly.

The waiter had no trouble keeping up with Dayre's rapid-fire delivery. After gathering their menus, he hurried on to the next booth.

"If we want peaceful conversation, it looks like we'll have to go over to Madigan's after dinner," Dayre noted wryly.

"You call this peaceful?" Kenna shouted as they walked into Madigan's forty minutes later. A rollicking Dixieland band was playing that night.

They left by 10:30. "Do you think you could stop by the office before dropping me off at home?" Kenna requested as they neared her campaign headquarters an hour later.

"No problem," Dayre agreed. "Feeling a little guilty about taking some time off for yourself?"

"I just want to check to make sure nothing earth-shattering happened while I was gone."

When they pulled up in front of the storefront office,

the old-fashioned half-frosted windows were dark. "Have you got a key with you?" Dayre questioned as he helped her down from the Bronco.

"Sure do." She reached into her purse and pulled out a chain with numerous keys on it. In the process of inserting the key she paused. "That's funny," she mused as the doorknob turned easily beneath her fingers.

She was preparing to open the door when, with a harshly muttered "Come back here!" Dayre jerked her aside and kicked the wooden portal open with his foot.

Kenna was about to make a sarcastic comment about the door already being unlocked, when she froze in shock. There was someone in the office—possibly more than one someone! She sensed their presence seconds before she saw their shadowy forms scrambling out the back door. A scream dried up and withered in her throat as Dayre lurched across the room to apprehend the fleeing intruders.

CHAPTER SEVEN

Dayre could only have been gone a minute or two, but to Kenna it felt more like a decade. Fear for his safety sent her heart racing and her stomach into a tailspin. During his absence she'd switched on the lights but instead of providing welcome comfort, the fluorescent illumination served merely to reveal the damage wrought by the felons.

Papers and files were strewn all over the floor while spray-painted insults adorned the campaign-postered walls. The wicker screen that had partitioned Kenna's corner office space was now leaning at a drunken angle while the two straight-back chairs lay splintered on the floor. Her lucky coffee cup, the one Meg had hand-labeled for her, was now nothing more than a pile of broken crockery.

"They got away!" Dayre returned to growl in disgust, breathing heavily as a result of his headlong chase. "The lock back there's been jimmied." Seeing the destruction that lay before him, he swore softly and succinctly. A moment later he had Kenna in his arms.

"Are you all right?" His husky question was murmured somewhere near her temple.

Hugging him tightly, Kenna nodded and returned the question. "What about you?"

"I'm obviously going to have to take up jogging. To think I was once on the college track team, and now I can't even catch a pair of common criminals!" The lightheartedness of his tone was intended to soothe her, and to a certain extent it did. The shivers that had threatened to overcome her nervous system were forestalled and her survivalist stamina came to the fore.

"Who would do something like this?" she cried in anger.

"I don't know, but I intend to find out," Dayre answered grimly, releasing her to untie the bandanna from around his neck.

"What are you doing?" she asked when he used the bandanna as a barrier between his fingers and the phone receiver.

"Calling the police." He punched out their number with the eraser end of a pencil he'd pulled from his pocket. "They like to be apprised of these things. Don't touch anything!" he warned as she moved to pick up a turned-over metal trash basket. "There may be fingerprints."

"What a mess!" she lamented.

The police, when they arrived, agreed with her. They questioned her and Dayre for over an hour while a technical team dusted for fingerprints.

The officer who'd introduced himself as Sergeant Cambell asked, "Can you tell offhand if anything's been stolen?"

Kenna mentally ran through the most likely items. The office equipment they had, such as it was, hadn't been touched. Their master campaign strategy report was not kept in the office. But what about other sensitive material, such as the financial recommendations provided by the Women's Campaign Fund consultant?

"The bottom drawer of that desk . . ." She pointed. "Is it still locked?"

"Frank, check it out." Sergeant Cambell barked out the instruction, which was immediately obeyed.

"It's still locked," came the reassuring reply.

"You probably walked in on them before they had a chance to steal anything," Sergeant Cambell told Kenna. "Have there been any other incidents of dirty tricks or political pranks?"

Kenna shook her head.

"What about the night your car wires were cut?" Dayre prompted her.

"The garage mechanic said that could have been done by an animal chewing through the wires," she reminded him.

"I know, but he also said that those wires could have been cut, that he couldn't swear to it either way."

The police sergeant asked for more details, noting dates and names in his little black book before concluding the interrogation. "We'd like you to come down to the station in the morning to sign your statements. We won't have the paperwork ready until then."

"I'll stop by in the morning," Kenna agreed.

"We both will," Dayre amended, shaking the police sergeant's hand. "Thanks for your help."

"I can't believe that one of my opponents would do something like this," Kenna murmured in dismay, surveying the chaotic damage after the police left.

"Believe it!" Dayre instructed her forcefully, watching her reach out with trembling fingers to touch the broken remains of what had obviously once been a special piece of memorabilia.

Kenna was caught up in memories. Meg had given her that coffee cup during the first campaign they'd ever worked on together. "You're going to go far, kid!" Meg had told the then twenty-four-year-old Kenna. "And I'll take this cup with me!" Kenna had returned teasingly, to which Meg had declared, "All the way to the capitol!"

"Be careful you don't cut yourself." Dayre's voice was gruff with concern as he carefully removed the sharp shard of pottery from her hand. Turning her to face him he said, "Come on, I'll take you home."

She shook her head, a look of grim determination shielding the turmoil of her expression. "I've got to clean this mess up. Until that's done, I can't be sure that nothing's been stolen." Beneath her jumpsuit Kenna's shoulders were braced, as if she were preparing for battle.

Dayre surprised her. Instead of fighting her decision, he dropped a soft kiss on the tip of her nose. "Then let's get started." His hand cupped her cheek, his fingers caressing her skin. "We're going to need help."

"I know that." Kenna regretfully moved away to pick up the phone and dial Marilyn's number.

"Hello?" Marilyn's voice was sleepy.

"It's Kenna. I'm sorry to wake you, but something's happened down here at campaign headquarters. The office was broken into and ransacked."

Marilyn didn't waste time asking for details. Instead, she promised to arrive with a clean-up crew within a half hour.

"Don't drive yourself crazy thinking about it," Dayre advised her after Kenna had hung up. He uncurled her fingers, which were still clenched on the receiver, and draped them over his hand.

"Did I remember to thank you for all your help?" Her question was directed to their clasped hands.

"You might want to save your thanks until you hear what other help I have in mind for you," he warned with a wry knowledge of her character. Kenna wasn't going to take kindly to what he had to say, he knew that. But he also knew that something had to be done.

"I'm afraid I don't understand," she murmured, lifting her eyes to his in confusion.

"I'm talking about increasing the security surrounding your campaign."

"Security?" Kenna repeated as if it were a foreign word. And indeed, it was a foreign idea. The need for security had not arisen before.

"What security arrangements have you made so far?" Dayre questioned.

"None," she had to admit.

His expression darkened ominously.

"There hasn't been any need for security," she explained defensively. "This is a local primary for a state seat, not a race for the U.S. Senate or House. It only affects this district and the forty-seven thousand people who live here."

"It also affects me," Dayre bit out. "You're more important to me than any damn election!"

"Don't scare me," she shot back, trying unsuccessfully to tug her hand from his clasp. "Don't make it impossible for me to function."

"I'm not trying to make it impossible for you to function," he replied, retaining his hold on her. "I'm just trying to make you see some sense. In light of what happened tonight, you're going to need security. The first thing we're going to do is call a locksmith and have all these flimsy locks exchanged for heavy-duty deadbolts. Then I suggest that a security guard be hired to watch the place at night."

"Only after the office is closed," Kenna agreed reluctantly. "I refuse to work in an armed camp!"

"Has anyone ever told you that you're indescribably stubborn?" Dayre growled in exasperation. He studied her mutinous expression before reluctantly agreeing, "All right, only after hours. But the rest of the time you'll have a beefed-up group of volunteers."

"What do you mean by beefed-up?" she demanded suspiciously.

"I've got a few friends who've been meaning to help out in your campaign."

"Wait a minute." This time she did manage to free her hand. "Are you talking about your hard-hat friends?"

He nodded, adding, "Don't tell me construction workers aren't good enough to be campaign volunteers."

"I didn't say that."

"Good. Then it's settled."

"I didn't say that either."

"Then what are you saying?"

"That I agree we'll need additional security under the circumstances." Kenna's gaze was direct as she

107

leaned forward to add, "But I will not be coddled or kept in the dark for my own protection. This is my campaign and I have to be aware of and responsible for everything that's going on in it."

Dayre viewed her determined expression with teasing respect. "I agree with you, so would you please get that murderous glint out of your beautiful eyes? We're on the same side, remember?"

"I remember," she answered.

"Good." His index finger saluted the tip of her chin. "Then also remember that I love you."

"I'm not likely to forget that either," she returned with a soft smile and a look that gave Dayre hope for the future.

"Good. You know, maybe you should marry me so that I can provide protection for you. Husbands come in handy for that sort of thing."

"I wouldn't use you like that," Kenna refused.

"Use me, use me!" he teased with a pleading expression that brought a smile to her lips.

It soon faded as the reality of tonight's fiasco shadowed her expression. "I find it difficult to accept the idea that someone is so determined to win this election that they'd resort to violence."

"It's happened before."

"But not here."

"Maybe not."

"What do you think they were hoping to achieve by ransacking my headquarters? Did they think they could scare me into withdrawing from the race?" Before Dayre could reply, Kenna fiercely answered her own question. "If so, they're in for a big surprise. I am not going to be intimidated. I am not going to allow

108

this episode to undo all the work that's been put into this campaign. A lot of people have put in a lot of time and money because of their faith in me and my abilities. I'm not about to let them down now. I'm not going to fall apart over this."

"Leaning on someone for a little moral support is not falling apart," he protested. "You're not speaking in front of a political rally now. This is me and I think I know you well enough to realize that what happened tonight was a big shock to you. The idea that someone meant to do you harm, whether personally or politically, has got to affect you."

"I'm not denying it affects me."

"Then don't deny that it frightens you."

"Don't you understand?" Kenna flared in angry frustration. "Fear is paralyzing."

"Don't you understand?" he retorted with equal anger. "I'm worried about you!"

"I realize that, but there's no need to be."

"Of course not," he agreed sarcastically. "The fact that your campaign headquarters were ransacked tonight by a couple of hoods shouldn't bother me at all. You may be impervious to fear, but I sure as hell am not! What would have happened if you'd been alone when you walked in on those intruders?"

"I wasn't alone." Despite herself, Kenna couldn't control a shiver of terror from feathering up her spine.

"But what if you had been?" he pursued relentlessly.

"Why are you deliberately terrorizing me like this?"

"I want you to realize the seriousness of the situation. Your safety is nothing to take lightly. You're not Wonder Woman, you know."

"Maybe not," she agreed wearily, "but there sure are times when I wish I were."

"You would look good in that revealing little costume," Dayre admitted with a smile.

Was this love, this warm glow he was able to light in her heart? "How is it that you always know what to say to cheer me up?"

"I don't always know what to say," he denied ruefully. "If I did, I'd have thought of something to persuade you to let me take you home."

And so it was that Kenna and Dayre spent their first night together—along with Marilyn, her husband, Ron, and a loyal group of supporters, all of whom were determined to restore the campaign headquarters to order. Knowing her campaign manager badly needed the rest, Kenna had delayed phoning Meg until early the next morning.

"What a mess!" Meg exclaimed when she arrived.

"If you think this is bad, you should have seen it earlier," Kenna quipped.

"This is bad enough, thanks all the same," she returned dryly, then it was back to business. "Is anything missing?"

"Other than my peace of mind—no, apparently not. We can't be sure, of course, until everything's been refiled." Pausing a moment to make sure they weren't being overheard, Kenna went on to quietly ask Meg, "Who do you think was responsible for this?"

Noting the graffiti spray-painted on the wall, Meg answered, "I think it's safe to say that the responsibility lies with one of our four opponents, or if not with them personally, then with someone in their fold."

"Which of the four do you think is the most likely culprit?"

"Off the record?"

"Off the record," Kenna agreed.

"Then I'd say the culprit is either MacCracken or Gordon. What about you?"

"I agree," Kenna stated, absently rubbing the bridge of her nose, a mannerism she adopted when she got upset. "Dave Frobisher is as honest as the day is long. As for Dickson, I can't see him jeopardizing his political future. This is his first election and the chances are that he doesn't have the confidence to try something this underhanded."

"Speaking of underhanded, I got an interesting call last night," Meg stated.

"More interesting than the one you received from me this morning?" Kenna asked.

"Aside from yours. The organizer of yesterday's seminar, The Role of Politics in Today's Society, called asking where you were."

"Why would he do that? The seminar was canceled. Wasn't it?"

"Apparently not. The cancellation call was a fake."

"Damn! That was an important seminar."

"Someone else obviously agrees with you; that's why they went out of their way to make sure you didn't attend."

"Did all the other four candidates attend?"

"Yes."

"I'll call the organizer personally and apologize for the mix-up."

"What are you going to tell him?"

"The truth."

The news of the break-in at Kenna's campaign headquarters made the papers that day. WISCONSIN WATERGATE? one headline questioned. As they'd promised, Kenna and Dayre stopped at the police station to sign their statements. Dayre then dropped Kenna off at home with instructions to rest, but she stayed at the town house only long enough to shower and change out of her wilted jumpsuit and into more suitable clothing.

Marilyn's diligent crew of volunteers had restored a semblance of order to the headquarters by the time Kenna returned. As promised, several of Dayre's hard-hat friends pitched in.

"I think this is a good idea," Meg stated.

Kenna, who didn't see the speaking glance Meg threw their newest and burliest volunteers, innocently asked, "What is?"

"Being provided with some protection. Dayre's idea?"

Kenna's nod was accompanied by a sigh of resignation.

"I wholeheartedly approve," Meg applauded.

"Then you'll probably also approve of the fact that I've hired a security firm to guard the office after hours to prevent a repeat of last night's excitement."

"I'm sorry this happened to you," Meg sympathized. "In all the years I've been involved in politics, I've never experienced anything like this. Oh, I'm not saying that there haven't been minor occurrences, character attacks, anonymous letters claiming ineptitude—that sort of thing. But nothing like breaking and entering."

"Not to mention ransacking," Kenna added, striving for a lighter tone.

"We're going to find out who did it," Meg promised. "I know the police chief personally, and I intend to make use of that friendship."

"Pulling strings already?" Kenna teased.

"You bet. These guys are obviously playing for keeps, so we should take advantage of every available resource."

"The police chief being one of your resources?"

"Absolutely!" Meg concurred.

Marilyn joined them, saying, "Kenna, don't forget there's another Meet the Candidate panel tonight."

After spending the day trying to catch up with her belated calendar of appearances, Kenna was able to fit in only an hour's catnap before getting dressed for the panel discussion. Her maroon suit was a favorite, elegant in design and flattering in style. Her blouse was a white brocade that slipped over her head and buttoned at the neck. Aside from her gold watch, Kenna wore no jewelry. Her hair had been freshly washed and blown dry into its usual complimentary style, her makeup discreetly applied.

Little did Kenna know that she'd need these defenses in her feminine arsenal to combat the arrows of discrimination she was about to have flung in her face. Not surprisingly, it was Buzz Gordon who launched the attack, accusing Kenna of sidestepping the major issues.

"My positions on abortion and gun control are both well known," Kenna stated, refusing to be intimidated by Buzz Gordon's obnoxious attitude. "What we were discussing is the need for more equitable distribution of state revenues in our district."

"I agree with Ms. Smith," Chuck MacCracken pompously declared. "Our district needs a strong legislator in Madison who will make sure that you, the constituents, get your fair share of the pot." He appealed directly to the audience. "We all know that government short-changes people, I just wanna even things up."

Kenna grimaced inwardly at MacCracken's "us folks" attitude. The man had a law degree from Columbia and had more money than the other three candidates combined. Why did he persist in promoting this image of a latter-day Huck Finn?

Dave Frobisher and Kenna both tried to keep the discussion on relevant topics, but they were outnumbered by Buzz Gordon's offensive attacks, Chuck MacCracken's longwinded oratory, and John Dickson's mistaken belief that keeping quiet was the safest way to win votes. At least you didn't offend anyone that way.

It came as a relief for Kenna and the audience alike when the floor was opened for questions. That relief became tinged with reservations when she identified the first interrogator as a reporter from one of the local papers.

"I'd like to get each candidate's reaction to the break-in and ransacking of Candidate Smith's headquarters."

"Did you hear MacCracken!" Kenna fumed at Dayre afterward. "He as much as implied that I'd organized the break-in myself to attract media attention to my campaign. And then Gordon's comment about women not being able to stand the pressures of politics. Ugh!"

Dayre guided her out into the cool night air. "Your answer put them both in their places."

"I know where I'd *like* to put them," she stated with intensity.

"I'm giving you a compliment here," Dayre maintained. "The least you can do is pay attention."

"Why are we going in this direction?" Kenna interrupted him to ask. "The parking lot is around back."

"I know. I thought you might be able to use a walk after all that political mudslinging."

"After being exposed to all that hot air, some fresh air would make a nice change," Kenna agreed wryly.

When they came upon a park with a playground a block and a half later, Dayre exclaimed, "Come on!" and tugged her across the grass.

Stopping at the swings, he ordered her, "Get on and I'll push you." Seeing her hesitation, he took her by the shoulders and sat her in the sling seat.

"This is ridiculous!" she protested.

"Now, don't have such a closed mind. Aren't you aware of the latest study that proved executives need their sandboxes, candidates their swings?"

"No, I must have missed that one."

"Don't see how you could have, it was on the front page of *The Wall Street Journal.*"

"I'll bet." Kenna couldn't even remember the last time she'd been on a swing. Surely it had to be back in fourth or fifth grade. She'd grown a lot since then, and her legs no longer dangled above the sandy ground.

Now they had to be tucked well under her to avoid imminent destruction.

Despite the logistical problems she encountered, Kenna had to admit that there was something freeing about being pushed on a swing. Forward and back, forward and back, like a self-perpetuating pendulum.

Dayre interspersed his pushes with questions. "Better?" *Push.*

When momentum brought her back to him, Kenna answered, "Much."

The next question was "Marry me?" *Push.*

When momentum brought her back, she answered, "Yes."

"What?" he yelled incredulously after his automatic push sent her forward again.

"Yes!" she shouted back.

Dayre took his life in his hands by rushing forward and using his body as a brake. The impact left them both breathless.

"Did you say yes?" he gasped.

Kenna expediently discarded words in favor of a nod.

He snatched her off the swing seat only to whirl her around in his arms.

"Stop!" Kenna pleaded. "I'm getting dizzy!"

Dayre returned her feet to the ground before asking, "Why?"

Although she thought the reason for her dizziness would be obvious, she answered anyway. "Because you've been swinging me around."

"No, why did you say yes? This isn't a momentary bout of lightheadedness, is it?"

"I said yes before you started swinging me around,"

Kenna reminded him. "So that rules out light-headedness."

"You could be lightheaded from exhaustion. You haven't gotten any sleep since the break-in."

"Would you please stop trying to diagnose me? I'm fine, Doctor."

"This is a serious decision."

"I know how serious it is," she chided him indulgently. "I'm the one who's waited this long to say yes, remember?"

"After twenty-four proposals, I'm not likely to forget," he retorted dryly.

"You've been a prince of patience!" she extolled. "And I love you for it."

"You love me?"

Kenna nodded.

"That's the first time you've ever told me that."

"It's not the first time I've thought it though," she admitted softly. "I've had all the symptoms for some time now."

"Then why wait so long to say yes?"

"I needed to be sure."

"And now you are?"

"I've never been surer of anything in my life!"

A full moon provided romantic illumination as Dayre stared down at her face, appreciating the intelligence of her eyes, the impertinent tilt of her nose, the soft kissable texture of her lips. His look told her how precious he considered each feature to be. With tender deliberation he threaded his fingers through the moon-lit strands of her hair, his communicative touch reflecting his love.

Kenna's eyelids descended slowly, blocking out visual interference. Now all her senses were free to celebrate the sensual pleasure he was evoking. The fresh warmth of his breath caressed her mouth a moment before his lips did. She welcomed him with loving eagerness, the subtle caresses of her tongue conveying the intimate nature of her pledge.

His groan of hunger was incorporated into their kiss, adding a new dimension to their passionate dialogue. The circle of his arms grew smaller as Dayre tightened his hold on her, molding her to him only to loosen her as he realized the incongruity of their location.

"A public playground isn't the place for the kind of playing I have in mind," he muttered, resting his forehead against hers. "I'd love to get you alone for a few days."

"Maybe that can be arranged," she whispered.

"When?" It was more a growl than a question.

"Right after the primary."

"Great!" He dropped one last swift kiss on her parted lips. "Leave all the arrangements to me. I know the perfect place."

During the walk back to the parking lot and their respective means of transportation, Kenna warned, "You do realize that MacCracken will accuse me of using our engagement to attract the media and draw attention to myself."

"I don't give a damn about MacCracken, unless he's the guy behind the break-in. In which case, I'll break his neck."

Kenna chuckled and cuddled closer. "I believe that's as illegal as breaking and entering. As you told me, these things are best left to the police."

"Then I hope they come up with some concrete answers pretty soon."

The mystery was solved sooner than anyone had expected. Kenna received a call the very next day. "Kenna, this is Dave Frobisher."

"Hi, Dave." She greeted him with friendly surprise. "What can I do for you?"

"This is very difficult for me to say. . . ."

The unevenness of his voice was disturbing. "Is something wrong, Dave?"

He cleared his throat and began again. "Kenna, it pains me to have to tell you this, but . . . we just discovered that my son Alex was responsible for the damage done to your campaign headquarters."

CHAPTER EIGHT

Kenna sat down before she fell down. She couldn't believe her ears. Fifteen-year-old Alex Frobisher responsible for ransacking her headquarters? Why?

But there was more yet to come, for Dave Frobisher continued. "After a great deal of serious soul searching, I've decided to withdraw from the primary."

"There's no need for you to withdraw from the primary, Dave," Kenna replied, shaking. "I have no intention of pressing charges against Alex." Pausing to catch her breath, she admitted, "I'm finding it hard to absorb all of this. Why would Alex break into my headquarters?"

"He thought he was doing me a favor," Dave answered with self-directed bitterness. "He thought he was helping me obtain what I wanted most in life—a seat in the State Assembly. And by doing so, he hoped to win my love." Dave's voice cracked.

"I'm so sorry about this," Kenna stated softly, hoping to mitigate the other man's obvious pain. "But as I said before, there's no need for you to withdraw from the primary."

"Yes, there is. I've been forced to seriously reassess my priorities," Dave admitted unsteadily. "I've been too wrapped up with my campaign. I haven't devoted enough of my time to my family. We've obviously got some serious problems that need to be solved. My son needs me, and I need him."

"Oh, Dave," Kenna murmured.

"I appreciate your not pressing charges. Alex knows now that what he did was wrong; that's why he came to me and confessed. He also admitted that he'd tampered with your car the evening we had that informal get-together at the public library. He's offered to pay for the damage done, both to your car and to your office."

"Why did he choose me?" Kenna wondered aloud. "Why not MacCracken? He was leading in the polls."

"Your views were the most similar to my own, so in Alex's mind that meant we would both be aiming for the same voters. If you could be frightened out of the race, then we would no longer have to share that vote; it would all come to me. That's part of the reason why I feel I have to withdraw. I want my son to know by my example that there are things more important in life than winning. Therefore, I'm going to be giving a press conference later this morning, at which time I will officially announce my withdrawal and my subsequent endorsement of you."

Kenna tried for another twenty minutes to dissuade Dave from going through with his plans, but to no avail. By noon the word was all over the district, and camera crews from Madison's network affiliates clustered outside Kenna's campaign headquarters. She hated the circus that was made out of one man's pain and her statement to the press was accordingly brief.

Chuck MacCracken saw Dave Frobisher's withdrawal and subsequent endorsement of Kenna as an act of collusion between Kenna and Dave. In an effort to combat the media attention lavished on the break-in and subsequent occurrences, MacCracken poured money into radio, newspaper, and television spots that showed him as a stable, family-oriented man who loved God and his country.

Besieged by the veritable blitz of advertising, Kenna decided to fight fire with fire. She had done her best to minimize the coverage of the situation with Alex Frobisher because it was not in her character to capitalize on another person's misfortune. But there was a bit of good news, aside from the promising results of the latest polls, that was yet to be announced. And so it was that the official announcement of her and Dayre's engagement appeared in the papers right before the primary.

Kenna and her entire campaign staff, which now included twenty-five people, spent the few remaining pre-primary hours glued to the phones, calling those voters from whom they'd already gotten pledges of support, reminding them to get out and vote, or placing new calls to tell people about Kenna and her position on the key issues.

"I think I've got a permanent crick in my neck," Marilyn commented during a brief respite in between calls. "It feels like I've called every single one of the forty-seven thousand two hundred and whatever constituents in this district!"

"Have you heard the weather report?" Kenna asked, taking the numbers of those who wanted to speak to her personally.

"It's supposed to be sunny and unseasonably warm tomorrow," Marilyn replied.

"Let's hope they're right," Kenna said before reaching her first caller and going into her spiel.

The weather forecast was right on target—sunny and unseasonably warm for September. The meteorological bit of good fortune promised to increase voter turnout. Kenna voted early in the morning, soon after the polls opened. By the time the polls closed she was running on nervous energy. Every available calculator capable of producing a printout had been gathered at campaign headquarters, along with bags of potato chips and cases of soft drinks.

"I thought candidates were supposed to rent suites in fancy hotels and everyone came wearing buttons and hats," Dayre teased when he arrived after his faculty meeting.

"You are wearing a hat," Kenna pointed out.

He doffed his Mets cap in a mocking salute. "So I am. Since I gave you my good luck cap, I had to go out and buy another one. Did you notice the button this one's sporting?"

Sure enough, there, attached to the side, was one of her campaign buttons. The red lettering stood out against the button's white background and looked very patriotic on the blue cap.

"All that's missing is the hotel suite," Dayre concluded on an outrageously seductive note.

"My campaign fund doesn't allow for extravagances like hotel suites," Kenna laughed. "Besides, as I've told you, this is a local race, not the presidential election."

"Ah, but the presidential election is coming up in

123

November. Just think of it, in seven weeks you and the President will both be on the same ballot."

Meg joined them with a jubilant expression on her face. "Do you have your acceptance speech written?"

"You mean?" Kenna could scarcely voice the question.

"John Dickson and Buzz Gordon have both conceded. A little over half of the total vote is in with Gordon getting less than one percent. Dickson got seven. They're both out of the race."

"How close is the spread between ourselves and MacCracken?"

"Our sources say he's got forty-five percent of the counted vote; you've got forty-seven. And those areas left to report are Smith strongholds. I'd say we should know the results by midnight."

Meg's prediction came within ten minutes of being accurate. At 11:50 P.M. Chuck MacCracken conceded victory to Kenna Smith. The results with 98 percent of the votes counted were MacCracken 43 percent, Kenna Smith 50 percent.

Kenna faced her cheering supporters with tears in her eyes. "This is not a bout of feminine weeping," she assured the crowd victoriously. "This is a salty show of personal gratitude to each and every one of you. Without your support I would not be standing here today. I want you all to know that I appreciate the hard work and long hours you've put in."

"Don't forget the long miles," someone yelled.

"And the long miles walking door-to-door," Kenna added, laughing. "And the cricked necks," she included for Marilyn's benefit. "The bottom line is that

124

we've proved involvement and determination can be more powerful than the almighty buck!"

Another round of cheering shook the room.

After a few moments, Kenna waved them to silence. "In keeping with my policy of directness and due to the fact that I'm going hoarse from shouting, I'll keep this brief. Tonight we've shown we can win the primary. Come November we'll prove we can win the election! Thank you all very much!"

By the time Kenna received the personal congratulations of everyone in the room, the office clock was displaying a time of 2:08 A.M. Since she and Dayre were leaving at ten A.M. tomorrow, no, today, that didn't leave her much time to sleep and pack.

As it turned out, excitement prevented her from getting much sleep anyway, so packing was no problem.

When Dayre arrived promptly at ten, he asked, "This everything?" pointing to her trustworthy piece of American Tourister luggage.

"That's everything. One case and a shoulder bag."

"I'm glad to see you're able to pack lightly." Picking up the case, he groaned, "I spoke too soon!"

"Surely a hardhat like yourself should be able to carry one teeny-weeny suitcase," she murmured in teasing amusement.

"Surely a feminist like yourself should be able to carry her own suitcase," he retorted in kind.

"I'm not a feminist," she answered, checking to make sure the door was locked. "I'm a moderate."

"You're a winner," he congratulated her, tossing her suitcase into the back of the Bronco.

"You know, I still don't know where we're going,"

she pointed out as they got under way. "You and Marilyn have been very hush-hush about this trip."

Dayre shot her a daredevil smile. "Marilyn is a woman after my own heart."

"She'd better not be," Kenna warned with a threatening fist. "Where are we going?"

Dayre's laughter was a welcome sound, and it made her realize how little time they'd had for laughter lately. "Guess."

"The Dells?"

Dayre shook his head. "Too near to home."

"Then how about Door County?"

"Nope."

Consumed with their guessing game, Kenna didn't realize the route they were taking. "We're heading toward the airport!"

"That's right," he agreed.

Her voice was curiously wary. "Why?"

"For the same reason most people head for the airport."

Kenna got only as far as the entryway into the air terminal before she knew she couldn't go through with it. She came to a dead stop, her limbs frozen with dread.

"I can't!" she whispered in a hoarse monotone. "I can't! I thought I could, but I can't!"

"What's the matter?" When she didn't reply or move, Dayre's voice became sharp with worry. "Kenna?"

"Get me out of here!" Stark panic was displayed on her face. "Please, just get me out of here!"

Dayre obeyed her frantic request, bundling her back to the parking lot and the relative safety of his Bronco.

126

He waited until she'd regained some measure of control before gently asking, "Now, do you want to tell me what happened back there?"

"I'm sorry," she apologized, still in a flat voice unlike her own. "I panicked."

"What made you panic? Are you having second thoughts about going away with me?"

"No." She reached out a cold hand to curl it reassuringly around his.

"Then what?"

"It's this airport." She shivered.

"The airport? Are you afraid of flying?" His thumb traced a comforting pattern on the back of her hand.

"Not exactly. My fears are related only to this airport." She paused to clear her fear-choked throat. "You may have noticed that I rarely talk about my father."

Dayre nodded, his expression clearly indicating that he couldn't see the connection between the two topics.

Taking a steadying breath, Kenna simply blurted the truth. "My father died in a plane crash. He was flying in from Arizona to visit me when his connecting flight from Chicago crashed en route."

Realizing she had to get it out of her system, Dayre didn't interrupt her.

Now that she'd started, she found it hard to stop the flow of words. "The flight was on a small commuter airline and information took a long time to filter through from the crash site." Recalling that horrible day brought an ashen cast to her face. "I waited here at the airport for hours. Waited for word, waited to hear if he was one of the survivors. Eventually they told me he'd been killed, and I haven't been able to go back to this airport since." By now Kenna was trembling almost uncontrollably.

Dayre's embrace offered her a healing solace. It wasn't a matter of simply holding her; he drew her to him, absorbing her pain. He cupped the back of her nape with the comforting warmth of his palm and murmured soothing assurances.

"It wasn't your fault," he crooned against her forehead, instinctively getting to the heart of her distress.

"Rationally, I know that, but emotions aren't always rational."

"When did this happen?"

"When I was twenty-two."

"But you told me you flew to San Francisco last summer."

"I flew from Chicago's O'Hare. I know it sounds crazy. . . ." she murmured with self-conscious derision.

"It doesn't sound crazy at all." He leaned away from her. "I can understand that the site of such a personal trauma would hold terrifying memories for you. And if you find it easier to fly out of Chicago, then we'll just drive on down to Chicago." He dropped a tender kiss to the tip of her nose. "It's only a couple of hours away."

"We can't do that."

He started the Bronco. "Sure we can."

"But aren't the tickets from Madison?"

Dayre waved away that technicality. "The tickets can be changed in Chicago. We're flying to Boston, so I'm sure we'll be able to find a flight."

"Boston!"

"That's right. You did say you wanted to see the leaves change color, didn't you?"

"Yes, but Boston!"

"Well, we're not actually staying in Boston. We're going to a secluded cabin in New Hampshire."

His description did not match the reality she found upon their arrival in New Hampshire. "You call this a cabin?" Kenna demanded, looking at the sprawling two-story building.

"No, I call this a resort." Dayre laughed at her expression of confusion. "A resort that rents out cabins. Ours should be that one over there, nestled behind those trees."

"The sugar maples?"

"The very same. Come on." He took her by the hand. "We'll go register and pick up the keys."

Kenna kicked off her shoes as soon as they entered the rustic cabin. "Alone at last," she murmured seductively while Dayre dropped their suitcases and hurriedly closed the door.

"What are you doing?"

"Shedding my political appearance." She tossed her suit jacket onto a nearby chair.

"How much wine did you have on the plane?" he asked with sudden suspicion, his eyes focused on the increasing show of cleavage her fingers were managing to reveal.

"I'm not drunk," she said. "I'm just pleasantly relaxed. Speaking of which, I think I'll go slip into something more comfortable."

By the time Kenna emerged from the bathroom wearing a flowing silk robe, the scene had been set.

The room was illuminated by the flickering flames of a newly lit fire in a natural stone fireplace. Dinner, complete with a chilled bottle of champagne, had been set out on a table for two.

Kenna was impressed. "Where did all this come from?"

"My luggage," he mocked.

"I'm impressed! What else do you have hidden up your sleeve?"

Her question provoked another of his famous "Who me?" looks.

Seeing that the verbal means of interrogation was getting her nowhere, Kenna reverted to a more direct approach. While Dayre was concentrating on removing the cork from the champagne bottle, Kenna snuck up from behind and slid her arms around his waist. Her fingers then concentrated on freeing as many buttons of his shirt as quickly as possible.

Applauding her height for once, she rested her chin on his shoulder so that she could keep tabs on her progress. Her fingers were pale against the dark bronze of his bare chest. There! Mission accomplished! Now she shifted her attention to the buttons on the cuff of the shirt's long sleeves. A smile lifted her lips as she brushed over the pulse at his wrist. She was getting to him! Once the cuff's fastening was undone, her fingers slid upward, beneath the cotton material.

The delicate raking of her nails across the corded muscles of his forearm so distracted Dayre that when the cork did part company with the bottle he was unprepared. The explosive *pop!* was immediately followed by a cold geyser of effervescence that soaked his shirt and skin.

"You're supposed to pour the champagne, D.J.," Kenna chastised him unrepentantly, "not bathe in it!"

"Dousing the winners with champagne is an old baseball tradition, and since you're the one who won the election . . ." He needed to say no more, although his threatening hold on the bottle did add an extra touch of menace.

"Don't you dare . . ." Knowing that was the wrong thing to say, Kenna immediately backtracked. "Wait! I'll make it up to you."

That caught his attention. "How?"

"Since I was indirectly responsible—"

"Indirectly?" he interrupted her to challenge.

"All right, all right," she conceded. "Directly responsible. Then it's only fair that I be allowed to repair the damage."

Dayre thoughtfully lowered the bottle from its previously threatening position and asked, "How do you propose to do that?"

Moving closer, Kenna cautiously aimed his champagne-armed hand away from her. "I need a little room to work," she explained.

"Work at what?" he growled as her tongue delicately traced his collarbone. "Driving me crazy?"

Her words were spoken against his bare skin. "I'm supervising clean-up operations."

"Say *supervising* again," he commanded.

Kenna did so, adding a "Why?" at the end.

"Because I love the way it feels."

"I'll make a supervisory note of that." She experimented creatively with a swirling lick. "You know, I've never had champagne this way before."

"That makes two of us," Dayre murmured huskily,

131

threading his fingers through her hair and guiding her mouth to those areas that needed attention. "No, not there, that tickles." Kenna added an additional flick of her tongue before he moved her over. "Ah, that's better."

"The champagne's all gone," she reported a few minutes later.

"There's more in the bottle," he suggested.

She leaned away to murmur, "Maybe this time we should be conventional and drink it from glasses."

"Conservative!"

"Hedonist!"

"You got that right!" He grinned. "But I suppose it would be a shame to let this lobster go to waste."

"What lobster?"

"The one under this silver cover," he answered as he removed the cover with a flourish.

As Kenna started to sit down, Dayre peeled off his sodden shirt and headed for the bathroom. "Where are you going?"

"To take a quick shower. Despite your attentive ministrations I still feel as sticky as a piece of flypaper. I'll be back in a minute."

"I'll give you five and then I'm starting on the lobster," Kenna warned him.

Exactly five minutes later, Dayre's voice came from behind the bathroom door to cheerfully inform her, "The deadline you gave me didn't leave me time to get dressed, sooo . . ."

Kenna heard the loud click of the door opening and darted an extremely cautious look out of the corners of her eyes. The first thing she saw were his bare feet planted on the carpet. Working her way upward, her gaze slid over the muscular contours of his bare calves, the classical structure of his bare knees, to . . . the dark blue terry cloth of a robe!

At that moment he formally announced, "I'm decent."

"Too bad," she retorted naughtily.

"Ah, is that disappointment I detect in your voice? If so, I'd be more than willing to satisfy your curiosity."

Dayre should have known that maidenly blushes weren't in Kenna's makeup. "You can satisfy me after dinner," she declared candidly, "because I can't resist this lobster a moment longer."

"What a blow," he sighed, sitting at his place across the table from her. "To be outdone by a crustacean!"

"Oh, I wouldn't say you'd been outdone exactly. I'm sure you and the lobster each have your own field of specialty."

"My field of specialty may well be to punish wayward wenches like yourself," he threatened.

Kenna dunked a piece of lobster in the flame-warmed melted butter and teased, undaunted, "Promises, promises!"

Dayre watched her eat the seafood, looking at her mouth in a way that made her hungry for his kiss. His brand of visual loving was addictive, she decided. Under the pretext of wiping the excess melted butter from her chin, Dayre swiped his index finger across her lips. The seemingly innocent encounter left a course of appetizing ripples in its wake.

From that point on, the meal became a tempting array of warm glances and teasing caresses bent on driving her to distraction. Kenna retaliated in kind.

133

When he stroked her cheek she ran her fingers across his forceful jawline. When he looked at her as though he longed to consume her, she promised him heaven with her eyes.

"You're playing with fire," he warned softly.

"We're playing with fire," she corrected him.

"In that case, let's go get burned!" He all but snatched her from her chair.

"Wait a second." She placed a restraining hand on his arm.

"Now what?"

"I've got to go change."

"You already changed."

"This isn't special," she protested. "It'll be worth the wait, trust me."

Dayre reluctantly let her go. "Since I'm being deprived of your company, the least you can do is describe this something special of yours."

Kenna waited until she was behind the locked bathroom door before saying, "It's a pair of pajamas."

"Pajamas!" he repeated in frustrated disappointment.

"They're blue," she added, as if their color would somehow make them more appealing.

"Great," he muttered, stalking over to the fireplace to stare broodingly at the flames. So engrossed was he with his own thoughts that he didn't hear the bathroom door open.

"What did you say?" she murmured, leaning against the doorframe.

Swallowing his disappointment, Dayre turned to face her. His politely stated "Great" was repeated in husky astonishment.

"I told you you'd like my pajamas."

They were pajamas, all right, but pajamas such as he'd never seen before. They were made of silk as thin as a sheet of tissue paper, and equally transparent. The top was a seductive relative to a camisole, while the bottoms lovingly clung in all the right places. She'd left the bathroom light on, so the illumination highlighted every curve of her body. The overall effect was much more arousing than if she'd stood there nude.

Kenna shivered at the loving hunger she saw displayed on Dayre's beloved face and the dark fire she saw flare in his blue eyes. This was the moment she'd been waiting for since the first time his eyes had captured her heart across a smoky room at Arnold's Pub.

She came to him, dispelling his fear that she was a vision. Her fingers were warm on his skin as she trailed them down from his collarbone to the loosely knotted belt of his robe.

"I think you'll find the wait was worthwhile," she whispered seductively, her nibbling teeth dazzling his lower lip.

Dayre pulled her to him just as her fingers released the belt from his robe. With nothing but the thin silk of her pajamas separating them, his hands closed over her tenderly, molding her against him. She arched closer, answering the beckoning promise of his masculinity.

From that moment on, each movement became a link in a sequential chain of erotic excitation. Dayre's seeking fingers slid beneath her provocative attire while his knee insinuated itself in such a way that her legs were nudged apart. Their provocative embrace made each overwhelmingly aware of the intimate differences between them.

Dayre was as responsive to her needs as to his own, his ardent wooing exciting her to breathless sighs of pleasure. He made a sensuous production out of visiting each of her erogenous zones and exploring them to the fullest, plying her with kisses all the while. His hands stole over her, from the talcum-soft skin of her back to the thrusting fullness of her breasts. At last, becoming impatient of even the thinnest of barriers between them, Dayre removed the camisole top, letting it slide down her body to lay in a pool at her feet.

Now his mouth adored what his hands had revealed. His teasing tongue and feathering teeth lifted her to the next plateau of pleasure. Kenna's hands tightened on him, her nails leaving half-moon impressions on his bare shoulder blades. Her head was thrown back; her half-closed eyes darkened with desire as she held him to her.

His caresses then moved with skilled direction, tantalizing her, approaching the heat of her desire. The building anticipation soon had her fingers on the move in a discovery mission of their own. She found him taut and ready where she was warm and willing.

Her distracting explorations signaled the end of his self-control. With a raspy growl of thwarted passion Dayre gathered her up and lay her on the bed. She was ready for him, her legs needing no urging to part for him as he levered himself into readiness.

They fit together with exquisite precision. She gathered him into her, her pleasure intensifying as she joined his rhythm. Now it was building, the pressure increasing until Kenna thought she'd go crazy. Then his skillful thrusts sent her right over the edge, holding him as her entire being pulsated with recurrent contractions. Dayre's answering shout of satisfaction was muffled against her mouth as he captured that moment in a kiss.

In the resultant afterglow Kenna could be heard to languidly murmur, "I hope the wait was worthwhile?"

Dayre's affirmative motion left them both little time, or need, for words.

CHAPTER NINE

At first Kenna thought she was dreaming. But this was no feather comforter she was snuggling up to. This was bare flesh and warm muscles! Opening her eyes, she removed her nose from what turned out to be a masculine forearm and focused her blurred vision on Dayre's hand, only a few inches away.

Even in sleep he'd managed to protectively enclose her in a loose embrace. His instinctive gesture brought an appreciative smile to her lips—lips that she pressed against the back of his hand. Holding his hand in hers, she turned to face him. The maneuver transformed Dayre's formerly loose embrace into a tightly comforting hold.

His sooty lashes rose, revealing sleepy blue eyes. "G'morning."

"Good morning. I thought I was dreaming," Kenna confided as she nestled against him.

"It's no dream," he assured her, tightening his clasp. "You feel very real to me. Very real, very soft, very sexy."

"You left out very tall," she teased.

"You may look tall but you don't feel very tall," he informed her, running his hands over her for a quick appraisal. "You shouldn't be so sensitive about your height."

"I'm not sensitive," she denied lazily, shifting her leg so that it intimately rested on top of his. "In fact, my height has come in handy in a number of instances."

"Now you've got my curiosity aroused."

"Is *that* what that is?" she retorted outrageously.

"Kenna Smith, you shock me!"

She borrowed his "Who me?" expression.

"What happened to the Pollyanna image of Kenna Smith, political candidate?"

"I left her at home." She toyed with the silky darkness of his hair. "Aren't you glad I did?"

Dayre nodded, but ruefully added, "It may take some getting used to," as her fingers explored him with artful abandon.

"It's too late to start complaining now."

"Oh, I'm not complaining," he replied, returning her fingers to their former playground.

"It's all your fault anyway," she accused him, tracing a meandering route from the tip of his ear to the base of his throat.

"My fault?"

Kenna nodded. "Being in love makes me shameless."

"Oh-ho, so you're in love, are you?" His voice exuded male satisfaction.

"Yes, I am. With a wonderful fella!"

"Fella?" Dayre repeated in incredulous horror. "This from an English teacher? I thought you'd at least quote Shakespeare to me."

"Shakespeare, hmm? How about 'Let lips do what

hands do'?" She suited her actions to the quotation, mouthing, "Romeo and Juliet, Act One, Scene Five," against the intoxicating texture of his skin.

By now Kenna knew her way around this inviting masculine territory—knew where a touch could be ticklish, where it could be energizing. Her lips skimmed over him, her tongue flicking out to administer tantalizing caresses as she showered him with kisses. She sampled the taste of his shoulder and compared it to the flavor of his chest. Her bracing hand rested atop his heart, monitoring his accelerating heartbeat as her teeth raked over his rib cage.

The attention she directed to his upper torso soon produced rewarding results in the lower half. Thrilled by this physical reinforcement, Kenna became more daring in her feminine siege. Part of her feared that Dayre would take control instead of generously relinquishing the reins of domination to her bewitching hands, as he was doing.

But her fears were groundless. Her lover resisted his own impulses and allowed her to enjoy the powerful intricacies of his body. His raspy voice whispered words of encouragement and sensual suggestions, spurring her on to new dimensions of love.

Her ears gloried to the sound of his pleasure. Her hands savored the muscular resilience of his flesh. Her mouth memorized the differing textures of his body. Her eyes feasted on the glorious strength of his arousal.

Incredibly excited by such prodigious power, Kenna lowered herself to him, completing their union with a deliciously erotic smoothness, testing the bounds of their capacity for pleasure. Words were exchanged for husky moans as the force of their love carried them away.

Only after the peak had been reached and their needs satiated did Kenna complacently challenge Dayre. "Still think men are more romantic than women?"

"The fair sex is certainly more innovative." The compliment was delivered in a velvety drawl.

"On behalf of all womankind, I thank you, kind sir."

"No, no. I should be thanking you!"

In the process of patting each other on the back, their hands were soon straying into tempting territory.

"At this rate we're going to spend the entire day in bed," Kenna warned.

"What a wonderful idea," Dayre decided, entrapping her legs with his.

They did indeed spend the day in bed, discovering and sharing.

"Do you realize that I haven't seen anything of New Hampshire since we got here?" Kenna stated the next morning.

"There's a simple cure for that," Dayre retorted. "We'll go for a walk. The resort maintains miles of hiking trails for their guests."

"I don't know if I'm up to miles of hiking," she said doubtfully.

"You know, now that I look closely, I think you're developing bedroom pallor," he diagnosed teasingly. "You need a brace of fresh air and some exercise."

"Thanks to you, these weary muscles are already exercised out," she stated pertly.

141

"In that case, we'll just take a leisurely stroll instead of jogging."

Their walk took them through the surrounding woods and provided endless examples of exceptional autumn beauty. Sunlight filtered through the dense forest of yellow, gold, and red leaves. Pausing at an old stone bridge, they tossed pebbles into the small stream below before tromping on through the chromatic carpet of fallen leaves covering the path. A while later they sat down on a small incline to rest.

"Thanks for bringing me here," Kenna murmured, leaning forward to rest her chin on her upraised knees.

"Thanks for coming," he returned. "I'm only sorry I put you through that turmoil at the Madison airport. I should have warned you we'd be flying. On a plane that is," he added outrageously.

She swatted his knee with a reprimanding hand.

He took her hand in his and played with her fingers. "Seriously though, I wish you'd told me about your father earlier. I would have understood."

"I knew you would," she assured him. "I should have said something, but the time never seemed right. Besides, I tend to block it out of my mind." She paused a moment to absently twirl a red maple leaf in her free hand. "My father never truly reconciled himself to having a daughter. You'd have thought my mother's death might have brought us closer, but it made my father even more unreachable." The leaf crumbled in her hand as she admitted, "I never felt I had his approval or love."

"Is that why you had such a hard time accepting that I love you?" Dayre suggested softly.

"No, I'm afraid the blame for that would have to go to George."

"George?"

Kenna nodded. "I told you I'd been engaged once before."

"To George?"

She nodded again. "When George swept me off my feet, I thought it was love. I was twenty-three at the time. Only by accidentally overhearing a few of his candid comments did I realize that the whole thing was an act. I was suitable; I fit all the requirements he had drawn up for the position of his wife. I was deficient in only one place, and that was in bed."

"You're not deficient anyplace," Dayre stated quietly. Mulling over her confession, he had to ask, "Is that why you've been so passionate with me? Were you trying to prove something?"

She stared down at the leafy remains in her hand. "I won't lie to you. The first time we made love I probably did feel that I was proving something." She lifted her eyes to his. "But you laid that ghost to rest. You've made me feel sexually confident of myself."

"You make me sound like a doctor."

"Well, Doctor, in the process of curing me you've given me another condition. And this one's incurable."

"Oh? What is it?"

"Love." She traced a caressing finger across the planes of his face.

"So long as I'm the only one who can create this condition in you."

"You're the only one," she confirmed.

"Then I feel it's only fair to tell you that you've

143

cured me of a condition as well." Seeing her confused expression, he went on. "Post-Watergate cynicism. I think you're going to be an extremely articulate and effective legislator, Kenna Smith!"

In grateful appreciation Kenna threw her arms around him and hugged him, tumbling them both backward into a pile of leaves. Dayre rolled over until Kenna was pinned beneath him. "Now I've got you, my pretty!" he crowed.

"You certainly do," she agreed seductively, moving against him with deliberate enticement.

His mouth swooped down to capture hers. The kiss was a textured seduction of teasing tongues and nibbling caresses. Kenna threaded her fingers through his dark hair, her hands lovingly conforming to the shape of his head. Dayre's hands were occupied with blazing a provocative trail from her shoulder to her hip, tantalizing every curve along the way. The sound of approaching footsteps crunching in the leaves brought them both back to their senses. Giggling like two children caught doing something they shouldn't, they scrambled to their feet.

"You've got leaves in your hair," Dayre took great pleasure in informing her.

"So do you," she returned, ruffling his dark hair with her mischievous fingers. "There! All fixed!"

"Allow me to return the favor," he insisted, wreaking equal havoc with her short blond hair. "Now, where were we before you so boldly threw yourself at me?"

Kenna restored order to her hairdo before answering. "You were enthusing about what a great legislator I'd be."

"That's right, I was. But what about your teaching position? Will you resign once you win the election?"

Kenna smiled at his use of the word *once* instead of *if* when referring to winning the election. "The district has team teaching," she reminded him. "That means I'll be able to teach during those times when the legislature isn't in session. I think keeping my job will help me retain my sense of perspective, keep me in touch with the real world."

"Excellent idea, keeping in touch." Wiggling a dark eyebrow, he added, "Let's go back to the cabin and investigate the concept."

"Marilyn warned me you'd only be after my concepts," Kenna sighed theatrically.

Dayre had the last word. "But what incredible concepts they are!"

Once inside, they didn't leave the romantic privacy of the cabin until the next morning, when Dayre felt it his duty to show Kenna something of New Hampshire aside from the resort's facilities. So they took a long drive in the car he'd rented from Boston's Logan Airport.

When they came upon a hand-painted sign that said ANTIQUE AUCTION TODAY, Kenna suggested, "Let's stop."

Dayre obligingly pulled into the long gravel drive that wound up in front of a faded red barn.

An hour later Kenna was ripping a check from her checkbook and handing it over in exchange for a pair of crystal candlesticks. "Aren't they beautiful?" she murmured.

"They're nice," Dayre agreed. "But I don't see why

you insisted on outbidding that lady in the flowered hat."

"These candlesticks were meant for us," she explained. "They called to me."

"They what?"

"They called to me," she repeated, running a loving finger down the fluted edges.

Dayre eyed her with guarded wariness. "What'd they say?"

"They said, 'Buy me! Buy me! Give me a home!' "

Dayre picked up the other item she'd purchased and mockingly inquired, "What about this porcelain chamber pot? Did it call to you as well?"

"That was a mistake," Kenna maintained.

"You're telling me," he murmured, studying the monstrosity.

"I was simply rubbing my nose, and the auctioneer mistook that for a bid. Winning the previous bidding war for my candlesticks made me excited, and I always rub my nose when I'm excited," she explained.

"Oh? I didn't notice you rubbing your nose last night," he stated with shameless interest.

"You're terrible!"

"And you love it."

"Guilty as charged," she confessed happily. "Can we take a look at some of those stands they've got set up out back?"

Dayre nodded, adding the qualifying rider, "Providing you don't buy anything bigger than a breadbox."

The first place they got into trouble was at the stand of an antique furniture dealer. The object—a parson's table.

146

"If this were stripped and refinished, it would be a real beauty," Dayre enthused.

"And you're an expert at stripping, right, D.J.?" Kenna purred, paying him back for mocking her candlesticks.

"I'm pretty good at refinishing too," he warned.

"Is that the part with all the buffing and polishing?" she inquired with a bat of her lashes and a dose of artless curiosity.

Dayre's appreciative shout of laughter brought the proprietor running forward. "Can I help you, sir?"

Between them, Dayre and the antique dealer reached an equitable agreement on the price of the table. After paying for it, Dayre said, "We're going to look around some more, so we'll be back to pick it up later."

"I thought we weren't supposed to buy anything bigger than a breadbox," Kenna teased as they moved on to the next stand.

"That rule was meant for you only," he explained. Pausing in front of a jewelry dealer's display case, he noted, "You know, we haven't had time to pick out an engagement ring for you yet. Would you prefer something modern or do you see anything here you like?"

Kenna studied the faded black velvet display case. "This one's nice." She tried it on. "But too small." She carefully put it back. Then she saw it! The perfect ring! A wide plain gold band with a diamond solitaire, its simple elegance a timeless reminder of another era. Would it fit? Yes! As though it were made for her! "What do you think?" she turned excited eyes to Dayre.

"It's nice."

"It's perfect! Don't you like it?"

"I'm not sure." He lifted her hand to study the setting. "I think this diamond may be loose."

Kenna's head joined his. "It doesn't look loose to me."

"Did I ever tell you about my Uncle Juffrouw, the diamond dealer in Amsterdam?"

"No, you never mentioned him."

"He taught me everything I know about diamonds."

Kenna's expression was decidedly suspicious. "Really?"

"Would I lie to you?"

"Oh, no, you don't!" she retorted. "I'm not answering that in a crowd full of people. Lord knows what you might do to me!"

Dayre released her hand with a practical suggestion. "If you really like the ring, we'll take the dealer's card and give her a call tomorrow. This is an important decision. I think we should shop around first to make sure we're making the right choice."

"I suppose that would be the sensible thing to do," Kenna agreed, reluctantly slipping the perfect ring from her finger.

They looked at the other stands, but neither one of them found anything interesting. Dayre had Kenna wait in the car while he went to pick up the table. Once it was stored in the trunk they were on their way, back to the resort.

The moment they stepped into the privacy of their cabin, Dayre announced, "I've got something for you in my pocket."

"Which one?" His outer jacket had numerous compartments.

"That's for me to know and you to find out!" he stated with an anticipatory grin.

Kenna searched all eight of the jacket's pockets but found nothing except two dimes and half a movie ticket. "You're giving me twenty cents?" she asked, holding the coins in her hand.

"No, that's mine." He took the money back.

Holding up the used movie ticket, Kenna joked, "You shouldn't have!"

"I didn't," he retorted. "That's not it. Keep looking."

"But I've searched through all your pockets."

"In my jacket, yes. But I do have other pockets," he blithely informed her.

"Well, if you're giving me carte blanche . . ." She peeled off his jacket and set to work on his shirt pockets. Both were empty. Her puzzled gaze slid to his eyes, where she caught his open expression of enjoyment. That look made her slide her hands lower.

"Hey, I don't have any pockets there!" he exclaimed.

"Sorry," she purred. "My hand slipped."

"Just make sure it doesn't happen again, at least for the next second or two!"

While supposedly searching his pants pockets, her attention became waylaid by the powerful body beneath her fingers. Unable to resist temptation, her nail rode the ridge of his hip bone with feminine playfulness.

"Any more of that, and you'll never get your present!" His warning was raspy with desire.

Kenna relented and moved her questing fingers to his back pockets. Aside from the tempting firmness of his body, she found nothing. She was ready to throw her hands up in defeat when she caught sight of the red undershirt he was wearing beneath his flannel shirt. She patted his chest for any suspicious feeling. . . .

"Watch that!" he cried, stifling a laugh. "I bruise easily."

"Ah-ha!" She rapidly undid his shirt buttons, whipping back the flannel material to reveal a pocket in his undershirt. Reaching in, she triumphantly extracted a tissue-wrapped object. "I found it!"

"Now open it!"

"I am, I am." She undid the paper and exclaimed, "My ring! You got it!"

She rewarded him with an exultant shower of kisses from which Dayre emerged with lipstick on his nose and chin. "I've put my mark on you!" Kenna's laughter was reflected in her twinkling eyes as her thumb erased the damage she'd done.

"You put your indelible mark on me the moment you walked up and asked me if I'd been waiting long. So I think it only fitting that I finally be allowed to place my mark on the appropriate finger of your left hand." Once the ring was in place and the pledge sealed with a kiss, Dayre looked down at his opened shirt and teased, "Now that you've half-undressed me, I think I'll go change."

"Change into something . . . sexy!"

Her mischievous command stopped Dayre in his tracks. "Sexy," he echoed. "Sure!"

Kenna was dreamily admiring the way the firelight was reflected in her new ring when he opened the bathroom door with much fanfare and a loud "Tah-dah!"

Her eyes widened and her mouth dropped open.

"I can see that my virile masculinity has left you speechless," Dayre stated modestly.

To which Kenna choked out, "It's not your virile masculinity, it's your underwear!"

To the red undershirt he'd added a pair of matching long red underwear and his blue Mets cap. "You don't consider this sexy?" he questioned with mock outrage.

Before Kenna could answer, there was a knock on the cabin door.

"Who could that be?" Dayre demanded.

"Probably room service," she replied, swishing past him and slipping into the bathroom. "Answer that, will you, dear?" she requested from the safety of the bathroom.

"Kenna! Let me in there!"

Imagining his expression of male discomfiture brought a huge grin to her face as she answered, "Not now, dear, I'm changing. Let the waiter in, D.J. Our meal's getting cold."

Muttering dire threats under his breath, Dayre grabbed the woven bedspread and wrapped it around his waist. He made one last bid to avoid the inevitable by requesting, "Can you leave the tray outside?"

"I'm sorry, sir, I need you to sign for it," a woman's voice came back.

In the bathroom, Kenna had her ear pressed to the door, hoping to overhear what was going on. The moment she realized their waiter was a waitress she had misgivings about her joke. By the time the waitress left and Kenna emerged from the bathroom, she knew by the size of Dayre's grin that things had not gone as she'd planned.

"What are you smiling at?" she demanded warily.

"Nothing," he said in a voice that meant quite the opposite.

"How did you explain your somewhat casual attire?"

"I told her you'd taken my clothes away from me, that I was a kept man, valued only for my sexual appeal."

Kenna looked at him in abashed dismay. "You didn't!"

"No, I didn't," he admitted. "But it would have served you right if I had."

"I've learned my lesson," she sighed with theatrical remorse.

"You can do your penance by joining me in the hot tub this evening."

"The hot tub! But that's outside!"

"So?"

"So, it's freezing outside."

"Not quite." Seeing her preparing another excuse, Dayre cut her off. "I happen to know that you brought a swimsuit with you, so just accept your punishment gracefully."

After dinner Kenna was still expressing her doubts as he led her to the waiting hot tub.

"You'll love it," he promised her.

She had a hard time believing that. "If it's so great, why is no one else out here?"

"They romantically decided to leave us alone. Okay, here we are. Robe off."

"Do I have to?"

152

"Yes, you have to." He helped her remove the thick velour covering, with him doing all the removing and her all the protesting.

"It's *toooo cooold!*"

"Then get in the hot tub," he ordered remorselessly.

"I'm going to remember this and someday I'm going to pay you back for it," Kenna promised darkly. There wasn't time to say more because a crop of goosebumps had already erupted all over her body. By the time she was immersed in the steaming water, her complaint had changed to, "It's *toooo hottt!*"

"Haven't you read any good books lately?" Dayre leaned back lazily, making himself at home by propping his elbows on the hot tub's rim and letting the water direct its attention to his scantly clad, muscular body. "Hot tubs have turned into hotbeds of seduction."

"What kind of books have you been reading?" she demanded, relaxing with much more caution.

"I'll give you the titles later," he promised.

"Don't bother. I won't have much time for reading, unless it's legislative reports and electoral canvasses." Caught up in the reality of work, she mused, "I wonder what Meg and Marilyn are doing right now?" Before leaving Chicago, Kenna had phoned Marilyn to tell her of the change in travel arrangements, but she hadn't had any contact with them since coming to New Hampshire.

"Probably wondering what *you're* doing right now," Dayre retorted irreverently.

"If they could see me now, decadently decked out in a hot tub . . ." The rueful shake of her head said the rest.

"You are not decadently decked out," Dayre corrected her.

"I'm not?"

"No. This"—he wrapped an arm around her and tugged her so close she was practically resting on top of him—"is decadently decked out."

Dayre swore afterward that what happened next was an accident, but Kenna stoutly maintained he'd planned it all along. Either way, the end result was the same.

In the process of pulling her closer to kiss her, his supporting elbow parted company with the side of the hot tub at the precise moment that his lips made contact with hers. There was no time to draw breath before they were both submerged.

Kenna broke away from him and broke the surface with a sputtered, "You've done it now!"

A second later she'd dunked him in retaliation. Their ensuing high jinks left them both soaked and ready to return to the cabin.

"Race you back," Dayre challenged.

"Okay. On your mark, get set . . ." But Dayre had already taken off.

"No fair! You cheated!" she accused him when she finally caught up.

Dayre closed the cabin door behind them and locked it. His blue eyes were alight with challenge as he said, "Prove it!"

"I'll go one step better than that," Kenna returned, her expression borrowing some of his mischief.

"One step better?"

She set to work on him before answering, "By unveiling the evidence."

"Your fingers are *cooold!*"

"Ah, but you're *sooo* warm," she purred, dropping his robe to the floor.

"And getting hotter by the minute." His raspy growl was caused by her advance to his swimming trunks.

When he wore nothing but a look of sensual hunger, she pertly drawled, "I see you've decided to accept your punishment like a man!"

"Wanton!"

"Most assuredly," she agreed, stroking him with appreciative fingers. "I used to fantasize about seeing you this way."

He wriggled his eyebrows à la Groucho Marx. "I'm more than just a hunk of masculinity, you know!"

"I didn't just notice your body," she maintained. "I also noticed your eyes." She dreamily gazed deep into their azure depths. "They spoke to me."

She ignored his teasing, "Like those candlesticks you bought at the auction spoke to you?" and went right on.

"I also envied you your sooty lashes." She ran an admiring finger over the spiky tips.

Dayre moved her finger to his lips so that she could feel his words. "One of us is decidedly overdressed."

"I hadn't noticed."

"Well, I have." And he immediately set out to rectify the situation.

"What about *your* fantasies?" she asked as he scooped her now naked body into his arms.

"Which one?" His voice was a husky drawl. "They range all the way from making love to you in the back of my Bronco to seducing you in soapy bubbles."

"The Bronco's in Chicago, but there happens to be an inviting sunken tub in the bathroom."

"And the bubbles?"

"In that bag over there." His look of surprise called for an explanation. "It seems that we share a fantasy or two."

Without releasing her from his arms, he bent over so she could pick up the bag, and then proceeded directly to the bathroom.

In no time at all the room was transformed into a Lawrence Welk set, with bubbles galore. Kenna and Dayre sat in the midst of it all, reclining in the sunken tub, up to their shoulders in piña colada-scented bubbles. Actually the water level was minimal, leaving more room for the frothy bubbles. Their hands were allowed to play hide-and-seek amid the soapy foam, although more seeking than hiding was being done!

Dayre's callused hands sought and found Kenna's luscious curves. The satiny slipperiness of her skin drove him to distraction. He couldn't get enough of her, and his hands returned again and again to ski the slopes of her breasts. They responded enthusiastically to his sporting play, their roseate tips pertly peeking through the shielding bubbles.

Kenna returned the favor, her slender fingers kneading the muscled padding of his chest, running over his ribs to playfully tantalize the planes of his stomach. Creatively painting him with the fragrant lather proved to be a particular favorite of hers. She found the feel of his rippling muscles to be incredibly exhilarating, and she expressed her delight both verbally and physically.

Meanwhile Dayre's finger play had progressed from

156

gentle teasing to hot tantalization until it had now reached the point of sizzling seduction. Kenna felt herself go limp as his gliding caresses lovingly prepared her for him. He offered her the promise of ultimate satisfaction, holding back until the absolute apex. Soft and slow, fluid and flowing, the sensual reality of their lovemaking surpassed their fantasies.

Her hips arched upward until he finally came to her, fulfilling her needs so that she could fulfill his. He rhythmically rocked her right out of this world and into another, a world where the reflexive shudders of his body were all she needed to feel; the indrawn harshness of his words of love all she needed to hear; the etched passion of his face all she needed to see; the fantasia of loving him all she needed to know.

By the time their passions had dissipated, so, too, had most of the bubbles.

"Fantasy number ninety-eight fulfilled!" Dayre's voice was heavy with satisfaction.

"I don't want this weekend to end," she whispered vehemently as he carried her from their bubbly playground to the softness of the bed.

But end it had to, with Kenna and Dayre flying into Chicago's O'Hare the next morning, where they were both surprised to be met by Meg.

Surprise turned to dismay when Meg showed them the Madison paper she held under her arm. The headline read: CANDIDATE'S FIANCÉ UNDER INVESTIGATION!

CHAPTER TEN

"Under investigation for what?" Kenna and Dayre questioned in unison.

Meg offered the newspaper to Dayre and an explanation to Kenna.

"The article says that Dayre is one of several professors from U of W's College of Engineering who are under investigation in a university scandal involving the sale of blueprints to blacklisted countries."

Kenna was having trouble taking it all in. "Blueprints?"

"Blueprints of prototype equipment the university was developing," Meg clarified.

"There must be some mistake," Kenna insisted in a shaken voice. "Dayre's name was added in error."

"I already checked that possibility with the paper. They stand by their report, said they had a confidential memo from the U.S. attorney's office confirming the story."

With a muttered expletive, Dayre, who hadn't said a word during their exchange, folded the newspaper he'd been reading. "I've got to get over to the university and find out what the hell is going on," he grated out with icy anger.

"I think it would be best if you and Kenna didn't drive back together," Meg stated. "The media have latched on to this story and reporters have been practically camping outside her town house and the campaign headquarters."

Dayre nodded his agreement, his expression closed as Meg whisked Kenna away. So the ranks were closing against him already. He couldn't say he blamed Meg. She was only trying to protect Kenna. His respectability rating had slipped noticeably; it only stood to reason that his acceptability as a candidate's fiancé would lower accordingly.

Candidate's fiancé. The words burned in his mind as he crushed the newsprint beneath his powerful fingers. The lonely drive back to Madison left Dayre with plenty of time, time to brood. Kenna had been ominously quiet after Meg had made the explanations. What had she been thinking?

His grip on the steering wheel tightened and he increased the Bronco's already unlawful speed. He had to get back to Madison and get to the bottom of this mess. Hopefully he'd be able to come up with something at the university.

But his visit proved fruitless. Everyone in the know at the engineering department had gone underground in an attempt to avoid the press. Those left were bureaucratic officials who were able to provide little information.

Dayre's phone was ringing when he let himself into his apartment. Hoping it might be Kenna, he sprinted across the room to answer it. "Yes?"

"D.J., it's Cindy."

"I suppose you've seen the papers." Dayre's voice betrayed his increasing disgust.

"I have," Cindy confirmed. "And it stinks!"

Dayre had to smile at his sister's characteristic bluntness. "You don't think I'm guilty then?"

Cindy answered indirectly. "Our parents did not raise a stupid daughter." Then she pointedly declared, "Of course I don't think you're guilty! They don't think so either."

Dayre ran a hand across the tension-bunched muscles at the back of his neck. "The folks know?"

"Afraid so. They read it in the paper."

"The Alaskan papers?"

"No, the local paper. They're here."

"What are they doing here?"

"Try not to sound so welcoming, son," Dr. Newport mocked from the threshold of Dayre's bedroom.

"I was going to tell you they've been staying at your apartment while you were gone," Cindy's voice informed Dayre over the phone.

"Thanks a lot," he murmured.

"Hang in there, D.J. Things will work out, you'll see."

"Thanks, Sis. Talk to you later."

As soon as Dayre hung up the phone his father drawled, "I see you've had a busy summer, getting yourself engaged and now embroiled in a university scandal."

"I can explain about that—" Dayre began.

"Which?" his father interrupted him to ask. "Your engagement or the scandal?"

It wasn't until that moment that Dayre realized how much he'd missed his father's uniquely dry sense of humor. No matter how tough things got, Jim Newport always had a way of putting things into perspective.

"I'm glad you're here. Where's Mom?"

"At the supermarket, buying the fixings for your favorite meal."

"Beef Stroganoff?"

Jim Newport nodded, adding, "You'd better not let the press know though. They might accuse you of being a Communist for liking Russian food."

Dayre smiled for the first time since he'd gotten off the plane. "It's good to have you home, Pop."

To those who weren't versed in family history, the casual paternal reference of "Pop" might have seemed incongruous when applied to the degreed Dr. Newport. But James Newport had grown up as Jimmy Newport from the wrong side of Milwaukee, and he'd never forgotten his blue-collar roots.

"Let's have a beer," Jim Newport suggested. "Things are bound to improve with the entire Newport clan here to work on it."

Talking to his father did help Dayre regain his sense of perspective. But all the good Dayre's father did was undone by a phone call from Larry Laruda.

"Where do you get off involving Kenna in such a mess, Newport?" Larry's voice had lost none of its clipped directness from their college debating team days.

"Where do you get off butting into other people's business?" Dayre retorted angrily.

"Do you have any idea what you've done to her?"

Dayre made a concentrated attempt to control his temper. "I would never intentionally hurt Kenna."

"The key word is *intentionally*," Larry returned, unimpressed by Dayre's declaration.

"What's your interest in this whole thing?" Dayre demanded.

"Our organization has invested a lot in Kenna's campaign. We want her to win this election."

"You don't give a damn about her getting hurt," Dayre charged. "All you care about is the election."

"I'm not the one under suspicion here."

"You're absolutely correct, as usual, Laruda. You're not the one under suspicion. You're the one making a nuisance of himself. Say good-bye, Larry."

"Wait a minute . . ." the other man could be heard to protest before the receiver was slammed down.

Hearing his son's selection of wrathful curses, Jim Newport inquired dryly, "Something wrong?"

Before Dayre could reply, the phone had rung again.

"Hello?" Dayre's voice turned the greeting into an ominous growl.

"Professor Dayre Newport?"

"Yes."

"I'm calling from the *Capital Times*," a woman's voice informed him cheerfully. "I wonder if you'd care to make a statement about the charges made against you?"

"No comment," Dayre heard himself saying. Only after he'd hung up did he realize that his automatic response might not have been the best one to make under the circumstances.

Hell, what did he know about sidestepping the press? He was an engineer, not a public relations man.

Isn't that what Laruda was telling you? an inner voice mocked. *You're a threat to Kenna's campaign.*

Furious with this feeling of inadequacy, Dayre disconnected the phone wire from the jack. He had to get himself together before making any other mistakes, not so much for his own sake as for Kenna's.

Kenna let the phone ring twelve times, but there was no answer. She hung up with a sigh. Weariness hung over her like a shroud. Had it been only this morning that she and Dayre had cuddled together in bed, safe within the romantic confines of their New England cabin? So much had happened since then. She hadn't had a moment to herself since she'd stepped off the plane in Chicago.

Now the pressure of thoughts too long dammed up threatened to break her control. Needing some peace, Kenna switched on her answering machine and turned off the lights. She sat curled up on the couch, her velour robe tucked under her. There, in the silent darkness, she went over the day's occurrences, bit by bit.

She and Meg had spent the entire drive from Chicago attempting to make sense of the situation.

"It's obviously a set-up," Kenna had said. "I know Dayre would never do the things they're accusing him of."

"That doesn't make it any less damaging for us," Meg had replied.

"This is all my fault."

"Your fault?"

Kenna nodded. "If I were just a normal high school English teacher, Dayre would never have been impli-

163

cated, never have had his name smeared across the headlines."

"They didn't actually use his name. They just said candidate's fiancé," Meg recalled.

"That's even worse. As if Dayre doesn't have any identity aside from me. Which is ridiculous! He's a highly qualified professional."

"Be that as it may, we still have a problem on our hands."

"All right, then let's look at this logically. Obviously someone does not want me to win this election."

"Agreed."

"Why?" Kenna questioned bluntly. "I haven't promised anything in my platform that would be a threat to any special interest group. Granted I've gotten a few letters of complaint about my position on gun-control and abortion, but you expect that."

"Whoever's behind this has gone through a lot of trouble to make sure Dayre was implicated."

"Does the U.S. attorney's office have any proof to back their accusations?"

"They're concluding a year-long investigation. The memo the papers got hold of is genuine. But until they're ready to hand down indictments, that's all they're saying."

"They can't seriously consider Dayre to be a suspect in this fiasco, can they? He's been working at the university for only a month and you said this investigation has been under way for a year. You'd think that fact alone would alert the authorities to the fact that these are trumped-up charges."

"The authorities are working under the assumption

that Dayre was the group's traveling courier. He has been in the Middle East within the past year."

"So?"

"So they're saying he used his contacts there to sell the blueprints."

"Meg, you don't believe these allegations, do you?"

Meg avoided answering Kenna's question. "The blueprints were sold to a country that Dayre did visit."

"Circumstantial evidence," Kenna dismissed Meg's statement with a wave of her hand. "I love Dayre. I'm going to marry him. Don't you think I'd know if he were the kind of man capable of something like this?"

Meg shrugged. "They say love is blind."

"Not mine. Mine's got twenty-twenty vision and it clearly tells me that Dayre is innocent. I want you to tell me you believe he's innocent too."

"I believe you, Kenna. If you're sure he's innocent, then innocent he must be."

"Good, I'm glad that's settled. Now we can focus our attention on clearing Dayre's name. You don't really think this will reach the point of criminal charges being filed against him, do you?"

"I wouldn't think so. After all, if this is a plan to thwart your bid for the assembly seat, it could only have been in effect since you won the primary five days ago."

"That's true. Had MacCracken won, implicating Dayre would have been a moot point. And I have a sinking suspicion that MacCracken is involved somehow."

"So do I," Meg agreed. "But the last time we felt

165

this way, Frobisher's son turned out to be the guilty party."

"There must be something we can do."

"Maybe we're looking at this in the wrong light. Perhaps someone at the university has reason to go after Dayre."

Kenna waved away that possibility. "He hasn't been there long enough to have acquired any enemies."

"Maybe someone at campaign headquarters will have come up with something," Meg had suggested.

But no one came forward with any instant cures. Marilyn gave Kenna the news that Joe Dileoni, their party's county chairman, wanted to meet with Kenna as soon as possible. The meeting took place over a late lunch.

In a nearby Italian restaurant Joe told her, "I've been watching your campaign for some time now, Kenna."

"I know you have, and I appreciate the advice and support you've given me."

Joe paused in his attack on a thick slice of lasagna to ask, "Do you know what I think is one of the more interesting trends in politics?"

Kenna, who was picking at a Caesar salad, shook her head.

"The sharp increase of women in the political arena."

Because Kenna had known Joe Dileoni for a number of years, she felt free to point out that this change had not come about as a result of altruistic slate makers deciding to field more women candidates. "It's still very difficult for a woman to get on the ballot for offices we have a chance of winning," she concluded.

"You've got a damn good chance of winning this election. Or at least you did before this unfortunate business involving your fiancé was publicized."

"Dayre is not guilty," Kenna maintained. "I'm sure the U.S. attorney will discover that when their investigation is concluded."

"I'm afraid we can't wait that long," Joe retorted.

"What do you mean?"

"Kenna, you and I go back a long time, right?"

"That's right."

"And I've never steered you wrong, have I?"

"No," she answered cautiously.

"Then take my advice now, and disassociate yourself from the situation."

Kenna laid her fork on her plate and looked Joe right in the eye. "Are you telling me to break off my engagement?"

"I think it would be in the best interest of your campaign."

"Wouldn't it look rather bad for me to dump my fiancé in his hour of need?" Kenna inquired with biting sarcasm. "Especially in light of the fact that he's innocent!"

Joe took her rhetorical question seriously. "I hadn't thought of it that way, but you could be right."

Kenna stared at the other man in amazement.

Joe squirmed uncomfortably. "Look, I know this has got to be a difficult time for you. Just promise me you'll think about what I said."

And so here she was, closeted by the darkness, sifting through her thoughts. But all she'd gone over so far were the political aspects of the situation. What of the personal ones?

She loved Dayre, that much was certain. That, and the knowledge that he was not guilty of selling top secret blueprints to a blacklisted country. But what could she be sure of in her life? The outcome of the election was now uncertain; the date of her wedding had never been set. Was it wrong to want both personal and professional happiness? Was she asking for too much? Would she be forced into choosing between her heart's desire and her lifetime goal?

Kenna's clenched fists punched the defenseless couch pillows. No! Damn it, she wouldn't be forced into giving up either one.

"Forced?" she repeated aloud. No one could force her; she was in control of her own life. Determination sent her across the room, switching on lights along the way. Ignoring the flashing message light on the answering device, she disconnected the machine and had her hand on the receiver to call Dayre when the phone rang.

"Hello?" she answered.

"Kenna, it's Dayre." His voice was curt. "We need to talk. Are the reporters still hanging around?"

"No. I made a statement late this afternoon." After her lunch with Joe. No doubt the party would be upset by her determination to stand by Dayre's side and proclaim his innocence. "The reporters have left."

"Then I'll be right over."

"Right over?" Dayre's apartment was a good forty-five minute drive, and then only if one exceeded the speed limit.

"I'm at a gas station a few blocks from you," he explained.

"Is something wrong?" Dumb question, she chastised herself.

Dayre apparently thought so, too, for he didn't answer. "I'll be there soon."

And he was. When Kenna opened the door she was shocked by Dayre's appearance. He hadn't changed out of the charcoal slacks and blue shirt he'd worn to travel in this morning. His tightly drawn features bore little resemblance to his normal facial expression. But his eyes were what worried her the most, for they were flat, devoid of emotion.

Kenna longed to fold him in her arms and offer what comfort she could, but her instinctive step foward was greeted by the lowering of an invisible barrier. Trying to keep desperation at bay, she invited him into the living room.

When Dayre chose to sit on a chair, Kenna perched on the couch across from him. "What did you find out about the blueprints?"

"Not a damn thing. I spent the day trying to find out what's going on, but no one was talking." He shoved an impatient hand through his already tousled hair. "All I know is that some very sensitive blueprints of a new type of solar engine apparently ended up in Arab hands. Several people in the engineering department are under investigation."

"Did you discover anything else?"

"Yes. That this isn't going to work," Dayre stated bluntly.

"What isn't?"

"Our engagement."

Kenna saved her panic and calmly asked, "Why not?"

169

Dayre leaped to his feet and started prowling around her living room. "I didn't know what I was getting into, being engaged to a political candidate."

"Oh?"

"I'm not cut out to make statements to the press," he said with tight-lipped anger.

"Who's expecting you to?"

"Are you saying I should let you do all the talking for me?" His anger was growing. "Do you expect me to hide behind your skirts?"

"No."

"Then what do you expect?" He was almost shouting now.

"The truth, the real reason behind this sudden decision of yours. And it is sudden, I must say. After twenty-four proposals you suddenly decide it's all too much for you?"

His jaw tightened ominously. "That's right."

"Bull!" Her hand sliced through the air in a physical gesture of dismissal. "And don't give me any garbage about the thrill of the chase! I know you too well for that."

"If you know me so well," he drawled with deliberate disparagement, "then you tell me why I've changed my mind."

"Because you're trying to do the noble thing."

"Which is?"

"Stepping out of the picture because of the supposed scandal attached to your name."

"There's nothing supposed about it. Do you know what this will do to your chances of winning the election? Destroy them! You don't need that kind of trouble."

"I need *you,* now more than ever." She spoke with quiet conviction. "We need each other."

He grabbed hold of her shoulders. "Listen to me."

"I have listened to you. I've been listening to other people all day. Now it's my turn to speak."

"Why are you being so stubborn about this?" His fingers tightened. "Can't you see it's for your own good?"

Kenna shrugged off his misguided logic by saying, "I'm allergic to things that are for my own good."

Seeing he was getting nowhere, Dayre tried a different tack. "Are you afraid of how it would look to your voters if you dumped me?" His question hit a nerve. He could see it on her face. "That's it, isn't it?"

"No, it's not!" she denied heatedly.

"Then why that look?"

"Because I thought you knew me better than that."

Weariness marked his face and roughened his voice. "Let's just call it quits before someone gets hurt."

"You don't think it's going to hurt me to lose you?" she demanded in sudden fury. "Don't you know how much I love you?"

His blue eyes ignited. "And don't you know that it's killing me to think that I've destroyed your dream?" he gritted out. "A dream you've worked toward for years."

"Dayre . . ."

He swept her protests aside. "It's time for me to cut loose," he stated with indisputable fierceness.

Knowing he had only her best interests in mind may have lessened her pain, but it increased her anger. When Dayre grabbed his denim jacket with the intention of leaving, Kenna reacted instinctively. As he rammed his arms through the sleeves her hands shot out to close the escape route. The clogged cuffs caused him to glare impatiently over his shoulder. Her act of resistance came as a complete surprise to Dayre, and to Kenna, if the truth be known.

"I'm not letting you leave like this!" Her words sounded braver than she felt.

His brow darkened in a scowl. "This is ridiculous!" he growled, attempting to wrest his jacket from her hands without hurting her.

But Kenna hung on. "I agree, this is ridiculous. So why don't you start acting reasonably!"

They glared at each other, more like opponents than lovers.

Stubborn fool! Each was silently deriding the other.

Dayre's mulish expression warned her that he was not about to be swayed by seduction, emotion, or logic, which left Kenna with only one option.

She played her trump card with a blank face that many a poker player would have envied. "If you break our engagement, I'll withdraw from the election!"

CHAPTER ELEVEN

The denim jacket fell to their feet like a gauntlet thrown between them. Dayre's blue eyes widened before narrowing dangerously. "That's blackmail!"

Kenna merely confirmed the accusation. "You're absolutely correct."

"Are you telling me that you'd actually withdraw from the election?" His question was voiced cautiously.

"Right again."

"That's crazy!" There was no longer any trace of caution in his infuriated inflection.

She replied with remarkable calmness. "Trading insults serves no practical purpose."

Dayre clenched his hands and gritted out, "It makes me feel better." Taking a deep breath, he asked, "Has anyone ever told you how indescribably stubborn you are?"

Kenna nodded. "I believe a devious carpenter mentioned it once."

"Don't you think you should listen to this devious carpenter?"

"I think I should listen to my heart, and so should he."

"You're making this very difficult."

"I'm trying to make it impossible," she admitted freely.

Despite his best intentions, his hand reached out to stroke her face. "I love you, you know that. I want only what's best for you."

"You're what's best for me," she stated with unshakable conviction.

Had the powerful male fingers stroking her face actually trembled? Her own fingers drew his to her lips, where she kissed the callused surface of his palm. Her loving gesture, small though it may have been, broke through all of Dayre's defenses and arguments, crumbling them completely. With a muffled groan more eloquent than words, he gathered her into a bone-crushing embrace.

Their need for each other was so great that they couldn't break apart. The moment was too intense for a kiss; only the limitless depths of an embrace could hold the entirety of their love. So closely aligned were they that Kenna could feel every beat of his heart. Her face was buried in the warm cotton of his shirt, her arms clasped tightly across his back.

How long they stood enveloped in each other's arms, she couldn't say. Nor did she care. This was where she belonged.

Their kiss, when it came, reflected a matching reverence. But adoring lips soon aroused strong passions and their caresses took on a new quality. Dayre's mouth engulfed hers, experimenting with slanting angles, exploring new tongue touches. The end result was nothing short of wondrous. These kisses were so satisfying in themselves that they opened an entirely new avenue of pleasure. Never again would Kenna be able to view kissing as merely a pleasant prelude to intimacy.

"Promise me you'll never try and leave me again." Her demand was delivered amidst a string of kisses. "Even if you do think it's for my own good."

He captured her wandering lips with his before murmuring, "I don't think I have the courage to attempt martyrdom twice in one lifetime." His blue eyes were brilliant with a heady combination of love and laughter.

By this time they'd adjourned to the living room couch, where they were reclining against the velour cushions.

Kenna traced a finger across Dayre's thick ebony lashes. "Things will work out, you'll see."

His husky laughter was a welcome sound. "I'm supposed to be the one comforting you, not vice versa."

She leaned away to threaten him jokingly with her fist. "Listen, fella, this relationship is a two-way street!"

"*Excuuuuse* me," he drawled, tumbling her forward until she rested on top of him. "If the little lady says things will be fine, then they will be fine."

Pressing her five foot nine inch frame against him, she said, "Who are you calling little?"

"Correction. If the feisty Amazon says things will be fine . . ."

Her kiss prevented him from concluding his sentence. Not that Dayre minded. Kenna had come up with some innovative techniques of her own, weaving dreams around him.

Time passed unnoticed, making him ask huskily,

"What time is it?" when they eventually came up for air. He was squinting in an attempt to see his watch, which was partially hidden beneath her head.

She covered the face of his watch with her hand and answered, "Time to set a wedding date."

"Tonight?"

"Yes, tonight. Amid all this uncertainty I think it would be nice to have something definite to look forward to."

He trailed a callused finger across her love-kissed lips. "You're an exceptional lady, Kenna Smith."

"I'd have to be for such an exceptional man to love me."

"That settles it then. We're both exceptional. What's the date for this exceptional wedding?"

"That depends on whether you want a large or a small wedding."

"You mean you're giving me a choice?" he asked in disbelief.

"Of course I'm giving you a choice. This is your wedding, too, you know."

"I do know." He stroked the patrician curve of her nose. "And I'd like a small wedding with just a few close friends and family."

Kenna nodded in agreement. "I feel the same way." She cuddled closer until another thought came to mind. "Is there any chance of your parents flying in for the wedding?"

"Actually, they're here now."

She moved away from him in surprise. "They are?"

He drew her back into the circle of his arms before saying, "They arrived unannounced while we were in New Hampshire."

Kenna fiddled with his shirt button. "Do they know . . ."

". . . about their son being in the headlines? Yes, they know."

"How did they take it?"

"They were upset, naturally."

"Naturally." Kenna could only imagine his parents' dismay at finding Dayre's name and reputation smeared with scandal. Would they blame her? How could they not, when deep down Kenna blamed herself.

Seeing the worried look on her face, Dayre sought to erase it. As was his way, the attempt was cloaked in humor. "Pop was the most upset. He thought the headline should've read Anthropologist's Son Under Investigation instead of Candidate's Fiancé. He settled down when I explained that anthropologist was much too long to fit in a headline."

Instead of smiling as he'd wanted her to, Kenna had tears in her eyes. "Hey, I was only kidding." He wiped a lonely tear from her cheek.

"I know," she choked, hugging him fiercely. "And I love you for it." What other man would have the confidence in his own identity to laugh off the newspaper's slight to his ego?

"So when do we celebrate the nuptials?"

"How does the end of the year sound?"

"Too far away. How about the middle of November, say two weeks after the election?"

"Okay."

"Hey, where are you going?"

"To get a calendar." She pulled a maroon date book

from her purse. "Let's see. . . . two weeks would make it November twenty-fourth."

"November twenty-fourth it is."

"Shall I write it down for you?"

"Shall I come over there and punish you?"

"Please do!"

Dayre made as if to charge across the room, then dropped back onto the couch. "I'd better not. My mother taught me that it was impolite to attack your hostess. She's looking forward to meeting you; both my parents are."

Kenna returned the date book to her purse and nervously rubbed the bridge of her nose.

Noticing her characteristic gesture, he inquired teasingly, "You're excited at the prospect?"

"*Nervous* would be a more apt description."

"Nervous? You? Why? You're smarter than a speeding bullet, more powerful than a locomotive, and you're able to lecture large crowds at a single bound!"

"None of which will necessarily endear me to your parents." She rubbed the bridge of her nose again.

He deserted the couch and joined her. "Hey, you really are worried about meeting them, aren't you?"

"Yes." Her answer was starkly honest.

Tugging her into his arms, he asked, "What happened to the girl-next-door type that men want to take home to meet mother?"

"You turned me into a wanton woman." Her voice was a pale replica of her usual tone.

"Come on. Seriously. What worries you?" In between each sentence, he applied soothing strokes to her back. "My parents really aren't that bad."

"I'm sure they're not. In fact, they'd have to be pretty special to have raised you so well."

"Tell that to my mother and she'll love you for life."

"Will she? Or will she resent the mess my political ambitions have gotten you into?"

"Why should she resent you? The headline wasn't your fault."

Kenna longed to spill out all her fears, but hesitated. Instead, she practiced an explanation in her head. To tell Dayre that he was under investigation only because of her candidacy belittled the importance of his own position at the university. Perhaps she was getting paranoid. Perhaps the entire College of Engineering was the target of the U.S. attorney's investigation and Dayre's name had been included only by virtue of his professorial position there.

But as the week dragged to a close, she was convinced of the political implications. A little research had brought several interesting facts to light, the most important being the presence of MacCracken's former campaign treasurer's wife in a secretarial position in the lower echelons of the U.S. attorney's office. Of course there was no proof, and the woman was in no way involved with the ongoing investigation, but Kenna was willing to bet her answering machine that this was the source of the leak to the press.

It felt as though the wheels of justice had ground to a halt as Kenna and all her followers impatiently awaited the outcome of the investigation.

"Kenna, Larry Laruda is here to see you," Marilyn told her on Friday morning. "He says it's important."

179

At Kenna's nod, Marilyn motioned in the handsome environmentalist.

Kenna put aside the speech she was studying. "What can I do for you, Larry?"

He surprised her by asking, "Are you and Dayre still engaged?"

"Of course we're still engaged."

"In that case you can convey an apology to your fiancé, if you would. I tried reaching him this morning, but there was no answer."

"Dayre's teaching today."

"I see. Well, I'm afraid I came down on him pretty hard the other day. He didn't mention my call?"

"No, he didn't."

"Oh." A flash of discomfiture passed over Larry's face. "Well, uh, that's not the main reason I wanted to speak with you." He regained his customary suavity, leaning forward in the visitor's chair to announce, "I got a sneak preview of tomorrow's front page."

"How did you manage that?"

"My fiancée is the paper's star reporter."

"I didn't know you were engaged." This had to be a recent development. After all, Larry Laruda had been a one-time marital candidate.

"It's strange, really," Larry smiled reminiscently. "Do you remember that evening you and I were supposed to meet at Arnold's Pub?"

"Yes." How could she forget? She'd met Dayre that night.

"I met Sherry there that evening. Her blind date never showed."

Was it possible that the two people she and Dayre were supposed to meet had gotten together them-

180

selves? The possibility brought a smile to Kenna's lips, the first all day.

"But I'm straying from the point," Larry apologized. "Sherry's contacts told her that the U.S. attorney's office will hand down indictments against three professors this afternoon. Dayre is not one of them; his name's been cleared."

Kenna didn't know where she got the breath to ask, "Is Sherry sure her source is reliable?" Her lungs felt suspended as she waited for his answer.

"Absolutely."

Sherry's sources turned out to be extremely reliable. The papers announced Dayre's innocence as brazenly as they'd announced the investigation. The U.S. attorney's office claimed they were doing only a routine follow-up on an anonymous tipster who had brought up Dayre's recent visit to the Middle East. "He was never seriously considered to be a ring member," a spokesman had been quoted as saying.

Marilyn clipped the articles and added them to the scrapbook she was making of the campaign. On the morning of November 7, the day after the election, Marilyn carefully entered another headline into the scrapbook. This one said: SMITH WINS BY A LANDSLIDE!

Meanwhile, newly elected Assemblywoman Smith's first unofficial act was intended to satisfy one exceptional man's fantasy—the way he'd helped satisfy hers! She'd planned carefully, enlisting the help of Dayre's parents.

On Wednesdays Dayre didn't teach, so he was free to spend the day with her. The as yet unknowing beneficiary of all these machinations had refilled the birdfeeder in Kenna's backyard, at her insistence, and had just left to pick up some hamburgers.

Twenty-eight seconds later he burst through the front door. "My Bronco's been stolen!"

"Stolen?"

"Stolen!" he repeated angrily. "As in robbed, swiped, ripped off! I've got to call the police." He lunged toward the phone.

"Wait a minute!" Kenna lunged right after him. "I've got something to show you."

"First I've got to make this call."

Kenna pushed the disconnect button. "Darling, it can't wait."

Dayre was startled by her use of the purring endearment, especially at a time like this—in the midst of Grand Theft Bronco! But as he was soon to discover, Dayre was in for an even bigger surprise.

"Where are we going?" he demanded as she insistently dragged him down a short flight of stairs leading from the kitchen to who-knew-where.

Instead of answering, she instructed him, "Close your eyes."

"This is no time for a game of hide-and-seek," he protested.

"Trust me." She ran her fingers from his temple, over his cheekbone, to the corner of his mouth.

He captured her fingers between his teeth, his hold firm but not painful, and subjected the sensitive pads of her fingertips to a demonstration of delight from the curled tip of his tongue. Only when he saw her eyes darken with passion did he close his own.

Kenna blinked at the voltage of sexual electricity coursing up her arm. Then, remembering her plan, she opened the door in front of her and tugged her fingers until Dayre was facing the proper direction. "Okay, open your eyes"—her voice lowered seductively—"and welcome to your fantasy!"

Now it was Dayre's turn to blink. His mouth dropped open in amazement, thereby freeing Kenna's fingers.

Their destination was Kenna's two-car garage. Or at least it had been a garage before it had been transformed into a scene from the Arabian Nights. The only illumination in the otherwise dark area was provided by flickering candlelight, set out on a long table beside . . . his Bronco! The rear tailgate had been lifted and the backseats lowered to provide a flatbed—*bed* being the operative word! Beckoning blankets and pillows had been artfully arranged into a seductive nest.

His startled expression compelled her to make an explanation. "You did say that making love to me in the back of your Bronco was a fantasy of yours, correct?"

"Absolutely correct," he confirmed with a still somewhat bemused nod.

"Well then?" She made a sweeping gesture with one hand. "I've merely set the stage. Does it meet with your approval?"

"Absolutely!" He nudged her forward and closed the garage door behind them, shutting them into the fantasy world. "How did you manage to get the Bronco in here? And where's your car?"

Kenna answered his last question first. "My car is in my neighbor's driveway and getting your Bronco in here was infinitely easier than figuring out how to lower the backseats."

"It was?"

"Uh-huh. I just used these." She dangled a key ring in front of him.

"Those are my spare keys! Where did you get them?"

"Oh, I have my sources," she replied airily, silently thanking Dayre's parents for their assistance. They'd been supportive and approving from the first time she'd met them, finally providing Kenna with the loving family she'd always longed for.

"Wonder Woman, right?" he teased her. "Did you make all this food yourself?" He indicated the laden table.

"No, but I did place the order to Eli's Deli myself."

"I'm impressed! And you brought out your talking candlesticks."

Kenna stroked the fluted crystal. "They're a matching pair, just like us."

"It seems a shame to waste all this food, but I have this terrible craving for something else."

"Something else? What?"

"You!" Curling his right arm around her waist, he pulled her close to his side and drew her over to the open end of the Bronco. "Shall I give you a hand?"

"I'd like both of them, please. Right about here." She pointed to her waist.

Dayre obliged, picking her up and lifting her into the cushioned interior. Joining her, he displayed the athletic grace that she'd always found so appealing in him.

Catching her staring at him, he asked, "Now, what?"

"It's your fantasy," she retorted mischievously. "You tell me."

"In that case . . ." Dayre disconcerted her by crawling over the blankets to the front of the Bronco, where he switched on the tape deck and flicked a switch that activated a team of hidden speakers.

"Won't the cassette deck run down your batteries?" she asked.

"Don't you worry about my batteries," he drawled. "If they should run down, I'm sure you'll be able to recharge them."

The mellow sound of "If I Were a Carpenter" filled the wagon's interior. When Dayre rejoined her in the back, he found Kenna smiling—whether at the appropriateness of the song or at his roguish humor, he couldn't be sure.

"Just to be on the safe side," he suggested mischievously, "maybe we should practice jump-starting my engine!"

This time her smile was just for him and he captured it with a kiss, his tongue rewarding the upward slant of her lips. He eased her down onto the blankets without removing his mouth from hers. Their tongues conducted a plundering discourse while their limbs became intimately entangled.

"Your engine's racing," Kenna imparted huskily. Her fingers toyed with the buttons on his shirt before sneaking in between the fastened edges to tease his bare skin. "The only cure is a complete tune-up."

"I think we're both suffering from the same ailment," he decided. "But I'll have to check under the

185

hood to be sure." He unbuttoned her blouse, revealing her underwire bra. "Yep, that's it all right." He unfastened the lingerie's front clasp and explained, "Spark plugs definitely require servicing."

Kenna playfully slapped his hand away. "My spark plugs are just fine!"

"I know a way you could increase their efficiency." He leered at her.

She tugged his shirt from his body. "How about your pistons?" Her fingers toyed with his belt buckle. "Are they hitting on all cylinders?"

And so they continued until each article of clothing had been removed in the name of automotive troubleshooting. Now that all material barriers between them had been stripped away they joyously celebrated by leisurely exploring each other's bodies. They lay on their sides, face to face, watching the pleasure gleaming in each other's eyes.

Kenna's fingers conducted a creative tour of Dayre's body, starting on his muscular back and moving up the indentation of his spine. Her hand then stroked its way up and over a shoulder to the valley of his chest, down the planes of his stomach to a trim waist and lean hips. She touched him as if he were one of the Seven Wonders of the World. Dayre responded vibrantly to her touch, his body quivering beneath her caressing fingers.

A ragged growl warned her of his waning control. In one swift motion he rolled on top of her, one muscular arm resting above the crown of her head, the other braced to her left. His lips bypassed hers, heading straight for the vulnerable underside of her chin. She arched her head back even farther, inviting his roaming lips to investigate the telltale pulse throbbing along her throat.

The pleasure Kenna had given him was returned tenfold as his hands and lips aroused her to a point of rapturous excitement. His kisses spilled over, down her throat to her collarbone. From there he was soon waylaid by a tempting pair of roseate peaks. Each surging breast was treated to a seduction led by cajoling lips and a reverent tongue. He mouthed intimate compliments against her skin, so that she not only heard the warm words, but also felt them.

He then addressed his attention to the tantalizing hollow at the base of her spine where the slight roughness of his callused fingers added a delicious texture to his touch. His gentle visitation to the heart of her passion brought about a tightening anticipation that escalated until Kenna was panting. "Please . . . please . . ."

With exquisite precision he came to her, his firm masculinity inciting her welcoming femininity. He rocked against her, setting a surging pace.

"Better?" he murmured against her ear as they moved as one.

"Much." Her voice was laden with satisfaction as she matched her movements to his.

Sensation built upon sensation, resulting in an explosion of undulating pleasure that left them both dizzy.

After his heart stopped pounding so heavily, Dayre said, "I think we've just discovered a new means of transportation."

"Mmmm, but you did all the driving." She ran a teasing finger around the circumference of his mouth.

187

"Is that a complaint?" he growled.

"Not at all," she grinned. "Just an observation." Her fingers began practicing a seductively slow magic over his body.

"That's good."

Taking his words at face value she murmured, "If that's good . . ." and initiated a roll that carried him onto his back, reversing their positions. "Is this better?" she purred.

"Much!"

LOOK FOR NEXT MONTH'S
CANDLELIGHT ECSTASY ROMANCES®:

All-new **Candlelight Newsletter**

An exceptional, *free* offer awaits readers of Dell's incomparable Candlelight Ecstasy and Supreme Romances.

Subscribe to our all-new CANDLELIGHT NEWSLETTER and you will receive—at absolutely no cost to you—exciting, exclusive information about today's finest romance novels and novelists. You'll be part of a select group to receive sneak previews of upcoming Candlelight Romances, well in advance of publication.

You'll also go behind the scenes to "meet" our Ecstasy and Supreme authors, learning firsthand where they get their ideas and how they made it to the top. News of author appearances and events will be detailed, as well. And contributions from the Candlelight editor will give you the inside scoop on how she makes her decisions about what to publish—and how *you* can try your hand at writing an Ecstasy or Supreme.

You'll find all this and more in Dell's CANDLELIGHT NEWSLETTER. And best of all, *it costs you nothing*. That's right! It's Dell's way of thanking our loyal Candlelight readers and of adding another dimension to your reading enjoyment.

Just fill out the coupon below, return it to us, and look forward to receiving the first of many CANDLELIGHT NEWSLETTERS—overflowing with the kind of excitement that only enhances our romances!

Dell **DELL READERS SERVICE—DEPT. B363A P.O. BOX 1000. PINE BROOK. N.J. 07058**

Name_____

Address_____

City_____

State_____ Zip_____

$2.50 each

At your local bookstore or use this handy coupon for ordering:

DELL READERS SERVICE—DEPT. B363B
P.O. BOX 1000, PINE BROOK, N.J. 07058

Please send me the above title(s). I am enclosing $_____ (please add 75¢ per copy to cover postage and handling.) Send check or money order—no cash or CODs. Please allow 3-4 weeks for shipment.

Ms./Mrs./Mr._____

Address_____

City/State_____ Zip_____

Candlelight
Ecstasy Romances™

$1.95 each

At your local bookstore or use this handy coupon for ordering:

DELL READERS SERVICE—DEPT. B363C
P.O. BOX 1000, PINE BROOK, N.J. 07058

Please send me the above title(s). I am enclosing $_____ (please add 75¢ per copy to cover postage and handling.) Send check or money order—no cash or CODs. Please allow 3-4 weeks for shipment.

Ms./Mrs./Mr._____

Address_____

City/State_____ Zip _____